michael dorris

the window

Hyperion
New York

First Edition

1 3 5 7 9 10 8 6 4 2

Printed in the United States of America.

This book is set in 12.5-point Garamond.

Designed by Mara Van Fleet.

Library of Congress Cataloging-in-Publication Data
Dorris, Michael.
The Window / by Michael Dorris.
p.   cm.
Summary: When ten-year-old Rayona's Native American mother enters a treatment facility, her estranged father, a Black man, finally introduces her to his side of the family, who are not at all what she expected.
ISBN 0-7868-0301-0 (trade)—ISBN 0-7868-2240-6 (lib. bdg.)
[1. Racially mixed people—Fiction. 2. Family—Fiction. 3. Parent and child—Fiction.] I. Title.
PZ7.D7287Wi   1997
[Fic]—dc21   97-2822

michael dorris

the window

BOOKS BY MICHAEL DORRIS

Fiction for Young Readers

Morning Girl

Guests

Sees Behind Trees

Adult Fiction

A Yellow Raft in Blue Water

The Crown of Columbus (with Louise Erdrich)

Working Men

Cloud Chamber

Adult Nonfiction

The Broken Cord

Paper Trail

Rooms in the House of Stone

For all my children, including Rayona,
wherever she came from

chapter one

chapter one

SHE NEVER SAYS GOOD-BYE and so I never know when she'll be gone. It's one of those things that you find out by its happening—like lightning, like the ring of a telephone, like the first smell of chill in the air that announces summer's over. Every time Mom doesn't come home in time for supper, I begin by ignoring the clock. I don't switch on the overhead light in whatever apartment we're renting because that would be admitting it has gotten dark. I sit by an open window and listen for the clip of her high heels on the sidewalk, trying to lift out that reassuring sound from the noise of traffic and sirens and the arguments on television programs or of other people in the building. I tell myself Mom has stopped at the store and will burst in with a surprise—lime Popsicles or a bag of popcorn or an ice-cold can of Tab—so I don't fix anything for myself to eat

1

because I don't want to spoil my appetite.

Sometimes I fall asleep still listening at the window and wake up later stiff and hungry, the streetlight making long shadows in the room behind me. I don't let myself imagine terrible things have happened. It's too scary to be afraid when I'm alone.

Usually, Mom comes home before dawn, her breath smelling sweet and smoky, and lets me crawl into her foldout bed as long as I don't crowd her. After such "hard nights," as she calls them, she sleeps on her back, breathes through her mouth, and the push and pull of her lungs is music to me, soothing and sure as the beat of the tide from Puget Sound. I try not to move as dawn flows through the window. I don't want Mom to turn on her side and get quiet. I don't want to worry that I am only dreaming her here.

The following day I miss school and Mom calls in sick to the restaurant where she waitresses on and off.

"I'm declaring a national holiday" is Mom's favorite joke, just between us—she'll make up a better excuse, like "family emergency," for my teacher and her boss. One of the rules of the national holiday is that we have breakfast for supper: scrambled eggs and fried potatoes and Froot Loops. Another rule is we paint our fingernails and toenails a new and matching shade. Another rule is we don't talk about the night before.

"Ask me no questions and I'll tell you no lies," Mom once said, and winked at me. "You know, Ray, it's like we're the same age but I don't know whether that means I'm eleven or you're thirty-two. Let's split the difference and both be twenty."

When Mom's that way I can't get enough of her.

But toward the end of spring I can't deny to myself that the hard nights are happening more often— first only on weekends, then once or twice during the week on a regular basis. If she's going to be "late"—by which she means she'll arrive home after I have gotten myself ready for school and caught the bus—she tries to at least telephone and tell me to have a good day and make her proud of me. There's always music playing wherever she's calling from and she sounds happy, in her party mood. That makes me feel both relieved and hurt at the same time, because I'd rather it was a national holiday for just us two.

Mom blames my dad, who's a temporary substitute mail carrier, for our unusual lifestyle. If he was more dependable, she says, she would have to be, too. Whenever he breaks a promise—like forgetting he is supposed to take me on a particular Saturday or like not calling until a week after my birthday this year— Mom seems secretly delighted, as if she's proven her point and now she's entitled to collect on the bet.

We have different opinions of my dad, Mom and me. She claims she loves him so much she can't stand him, that we're lucky he's out of our lives for good but when the hell is he coming back, that he's the only halfway decent man on earth and yet he's a no-good loser.

Me, I just miss him. Mom's from Montana— "pure Indian," she brags—but Dad's more mysterious: dark complected, sharp cologne, sad pale-green eyes. His skin feels like satin, which Mom says is no fair because he doesn't even have to use moisturizer to get the effect. I don't see that much of him and when he does show up Mom wants him to herself, sends me to the store to buy stuff we don't need, already have, tells me not to be in a rush because I'll get run over in traffic.

But I do rush. I want to be with him as much as she does and whenever I walk in he seems glad to see me. He'll be smiling, pointing at me as though I'm a pleasant surprise, while Mom is shooting me dirty looks and thinking how to get rid of me next.

Sooner or later it has to happen. Mom is in the third day of her latest hard night—I have no idea where she is—and out of the blue Dad's knocking at the door.

"Hey, baby," he says when I slide the chain off the lock. "Where's Christine hiding herself?"

The shock of his presence throws me off, ties my tongue, and that hesitation clues Dad that some-thing's not right. He opens the refrigerator and finds it's almost empty because Mom hasn't been back since she got her paycheck.

"How long?" he asks me.

"I don't know," I tell him. "Not long."

"When did you eat last?"

"I eat all the time. That's why there's nothing in there." I point to the fridge. Its door is still standing open. "I made a pig of myself."

Dad gives me a look—his eyes are the color of the water at the Seattle aquarium, where we go once a year on a school trip. A manta ray could glide across his gaze any minute.

"Come on," he says, and we're out of the apart-ment, down three flights of stairs, and on the street. Dad spots an International House of Pancakes two blocks north and we head for it. It's full of Indians— a local hangout where hard cases and reservation types in town to visit relatives sick at the Indian Health Service Hospital eat plates full of Belgian waffles covered by mountains of whipped cream spritzed from red-and-white cans.

Everything on the menu looks good to me but I don't want to let on that I'm that hungry. "Just toast," I say.

There are those eyes again. I can almost imagine

a little sign next to them that describes the many forms of life found in an ordinary pond.

"Toast," Dad says as if the idea disgusts him, and then tries to charm the waitress when she comes over.

"Good morning, pretty lady," he croons, all bright and sparkly.

The woman, who's been hearing stuff like this since her shift started at six, just flips her order book and waits. She doesn't even particularly register that Dad's black, out of place, and drawing an occasional glance of curiosity from the other customers.

The waitress, named Marie according to her name tag, taps her pencil. She doesn't have all day.

"My date here will have the number six," Dad says, refusing to give up. "And I . . . what do *you* recommend . . . Marie?"

He can't turn himself off. It's amazing.

"Anything that's expensive," Marie tells him. "Fifteen percent gratuity is automatically added to your bill."

"I always tip twenty," Dad tries.

"Big spender." But then she sees from Dad's postal uniform that he probably truly is employed, and she softens. "How about the steak and eggs, with silver dollars on the side, sourdough toast, fresh squeezed, and coffee?"

"Whatever you say. But bring lots of sugar and

syrup. I like my sweets."

Marie can't help it: she smiles at the same time she rolls her eyes to the ceiling.

"She goes for me," Dad confides, pleased with himself, when she places our orders.

I look back at the menu and discover that the number six is something called the Space Needle—a pile of six fluffy buttermilk pancakes, each one made with a different extra ingredient: blueberries, strawberries, chocolate chips, loganberries, Washington cherries, and pineapple. It sounds wonderful.

Now that we're alone, Dad focuses his attention on me. He starts out with small talk.

"How's school?"

I look at Dad before I answer, but he's watching Marie. I feel like giving him a surprise quiz to see what he knows about me. What grade am I in? I could ask him. Which school do I go to? Who's my teacher? What's my favorite subject? Would he guess right? Fifth, Melrose, Ms. Cohen? Would he know that I like to draw maps, read *Star Trek* books, or that I wish more than anything I had a best friend? Do I really want to find out what he doesn't know?

"Okay," I tell him. "School's okay. It's over for the summer tomorrow, anyway."

"Great, great, baby," Dad says, his eyes roaming the restaurant.

"Look at me!" I want to yell, but don't.

Now he gets to the subject he's interested in.

"So where is she?"

"She had to be at work early."

"Uh-huh."

"Really, Dad."

"This can't keep up, Rayona. You know that, right?"

"What can't?" I'm beginning to panic.

"I've got to take some responsibility. I am your father."

He's actually about to invite me to live with him. I can't believe what I'm hearing. But it's not impossible. One other time, when Mom went to voluntary in-house treatment—she lasted just two days because she said the other patients drove her crazy with their "war stories"—I stayed with Dad at his apartment. We ate take-out sweet-and-sour pork and went to two movies in one day. He even took me to the post office and introduced me to some of the people he worked with. *"Daughter?"* one of them joked. "Elgin, do you know who the mother is?" Still, at the thought of staying with Dad again I'm excited, thrilled. But who'll watch out for Mom?

"I'm going to call Social Services," Dad continues. "I know a lady there who owes me big time. She'll find you a good placement."

He must see the expression on my face.

"Just temporary, baby. Till your mom puts it together again." He actually pats my hand, which smears the purple crayon I'm using to press color into the child's menu the waitress set before me before she knew I was a candidate for the Space Needle.

"I can take care of myself."

"None of us can do that all the time." Dad, of course, is talking about himself now. Or Mom. Or whoever. The difference is, I can. My parents are more of a problem to me than I am to them.

There's no convincing Dad of that, though. I halfway wonder if I'm just his excuse to call this lady he knows, a suspicion that grows when I overhear his end of the conversation he has with her from the House of Pancakes pay phone.

"Irene," he says. "Guess who?" Then immediately, "No, don't hang up, angel, this is business. This is serious. It's about my daughter."

Long silence while Irene absorbs this news.

"Sure I told you." Dad gives me an expression that says, "Don't blame me." "It was a long time ago. Way before us."

Mom would love to hear that.

"Ten at least."

Come on, Dad, you just missed my birthday.

"See, her mom's got a problem, you know, and Ray, my daughter, needs somewhere to crash for a

9

while till she—her mom—dries out."

Tell her all our secrets, why don't you? I don't like Irene already.

"I'd consider it a favor," Dad says. "A *personal* favor."

He always uses bait on his hook.

"Sure, Friday night's cool. Payback time."

He smiles, hangs up, turns to me, Mr. Success. "It's all set. Just pack a bag—you don't need much. I'll crash with you at the apartment tonight, then take you over to her office after school tomorrow. Perfect timing, with vacation and all. And Irene will know just the right family for you."

I glare at him. "I guess that's because you told her so much about me."

"Don't mouth," Dad says. "This is for the best. And just for a few days. I'll track down Christine and get her on her feet. You being with Social Services will wake her up fast. Whatever else, she loves you, baby."

"I'm not a baby."

"You'll always be *my* baby. I remember that first time I saw you in the hospital, so tiny and brown—"

"How old was I the next time you saw me?"

"Ray." Dad acts all hurt. "Don't judge. Adult stuff is messy. Someday you'll understand."

That's the trouble with being a kid: grown-ups say things to you and you can't be sure they're wrong. It just leaves you feeling stupid and helpless.

"So who's this perfect family?"

Dad is at a loss. "Irene's an expert," he explains. "She knows her business. Trust me."

Irene, when we meet at her office late in the afternoon, turns out to be older than I expect. Older than Dad's usual women friends. She's a short version of that actress who plays a nurse on TV, is dressed in a green suit, and has spent a lot of attention on her fingernails. She wears dangly earrings and a heavy gold necklace, and she smells like lemons. She pointedly ignores Dad and makes a big deal of coming around her desk and stooping down directly in front of me.

"What's your name, sweetheart?"

"Rayona Diane Taylor."

"Ma'am," Dad, ever worried about being polite, adds for me.

I can ignore him, too.

"Do you know where your mama is?" Irene asks.

"She's out," I say. "At work, probably."

"Ma'am."

"Um-hum," Irene Baker says. I can tell she knows something I don't.

"She always comes back."

"I believe you, honey. It's my job to be sure that you're in good hands till she does. I did a little checking today and"—here she hesitates, about to make her big announcement—"and the good news is that your mama? She's getting the help she needs. A full twenty-eight-day mandated program. No cost to her whatsoever. The county is taking care of it. Good nutrition, counseling, a stable environment. You won't know her when she's done. She'll be a new woman. Serene."

Irene looks at me closely to see how I react to this news. As far as she's concerned, Dad is on another planet. "Your mama," she begins, then asks a question to which she already has figured out the answer: "She's not black, is she?"

"No."

"Ma'am."

"That complicates things a little." Irene pretends to bite on one of her expensive nails. "Would you be more comfortable in a white home or with a black family?"

I could have told her right then that Mom was Indian, but I want to know something this Irene doesn't—besides the fact that it will take more than twenty-eight days to make Mom "serene"—so before Dad fills her in I say the last thing he hopes to hear.

"White."

Finally Irene gives him a look, and it isn't friendly.

"That's perfectly all right," she says to me as if I

have just spilled a glass of milk in her clean kitchen. "Let me make a few calls. We'll do this out of court like you wanted, Elgin," she says to my dad, "but if there are any screwups I'm going to have your jive head on a plate."

"Ray's going to cooperate," Dad promises Irene. "She's a winner. Takes after her old man."

"What do you mean by 'screwup'?" I ask Irene, trying to sound innocent and sincere, but she just bats her eyes, slowly. I can use all the ideas for escape I can get. I see the plate in my mind—gold like in King Herod's court, maybe with one of those domed things over the top of it. I lift the lid and there's Dad, all sorry for himself.

"Rayona," his head says to me. "I'm sorry. I don't know why I didn't think of taking you myself."

I replace the lid, cut him off. He had his chance.

chapter two
chapter two

"THE POTTERS" READS A HOMEMADE sign bordered by stenciled blue flowers and little Disney bunnies and ducks. The sign is nailed next to the aluminum door of an aluminum prefab house that is exactly the same as every other house in this development near Renton. Well, there are, to be honest, a few differences. Some houses have flower boxes filled with fake geraniums. Some have twirling weather vanes on their roofs. Some have fancy wrought-iron knockers instead of doorbells. This one has the sign.

"Now, Rayona." Irene pauses before the aluminum steps. "Do you remember all I've told you?"

You only repeated it six times while I tried to eat a grilled-cheese sandwich for supper, I am tempted to answer, but why bother? So I play back the tape.

"Frieda and Bill," I recite. "He sells cars, she's a homemaker. Two kids of their own, both older than me."

Irene's shiny face looks stricken. I have forgotten some detail.

"Ben is twenty and has a job at Sea-Tac," I put her mind at rest. "Brian is seventeen and a senior in high school."

She's satisfied, so I continue. "Dog named Roger, bird . . . "

"Potty," Irene helps me out.

"They have a great record of taking in kids like me on a short-term basis. I play by the rules and we'll get along fine."

Irene nods but doesn't buy my act. "Look, Ray," she says, her manicured hand on my shoulder. The claws could dig in at any moment and they look sharp to me. "You are Elgin Taylor's daughter, which means you must have inherited at least some of his fatal charm. I've got two words of advice for you: use it."

Just as I feel the pressure of her fingernails bear down on my skin, the door opens and there, as if they were posed in a Christmas-card family photo, are The Potters. They fill the space. Ben and Brian on either side of Frieda and Bill, Roger trying to get out to lick me. At least the bird's missing.

"Come in and meet Potty," they all seem to cry at the same time. "You must be Ray Ann."

You wouldn't think there could be such a thing as too nice, but in fact "too" anything can drive you crazy. All the Potters, human or otherwise, fall over themselves to let me know how glad they are to see me. They make it seem as though there has been this big vacuum in their lives and I am the one to occupy it. I can tell instantly that they're not going to make it easy for me to screw up.

"Here is your room." How is it that they can all say the same thing at the same time? It's like listening to the Doublemint Twins, except they've become quadruplets.

"My" room is, I have to admit, pretty great. A bed with a frilly spread. A dresser. A desk and a chair made out of some kind of wood. A bookshelf with four Nancy Drews and four Hardy Boys. Even the bird.

"We put Potty in here to keep you company, if that's all right," Bill Potter tells me.

"If it's not, if you're allergic to feathers or saw that Alfred Hitchcock movie, we'll understand," Frieda Potter adds.

"His feelings won't be hurt a bit," Ben Potter assures me.

"But he can talk," Brian Potter finishes. "He's trained."

Do I want a bird? Do I want to disappoint The Potters, who are all leaning forward, breathlessly waiting for my decision? For a flash I picture Mom standing here beside me. I try to imagine what sarcastic crack she would whisper in my ear to give me a handle on what to think. I listen hard, waiting for her clue, but she's quiet for once. I'm on my own, and so I do the dumbest, most embarrassing thing.

I start to cry.

If The Potters—and that's how I can't help but think of them, as if they're all parts of one giant, gentle creature—were nice before, the sight of my tears turns up the volume of their concern for my happiness. We're talking hot chocolate made from real milk warmed in a pan on the top of the stove. We're talking bubble bath. We're talking an actual nightgown—me, who's always slept in Mom's old T-shirts—that's been ironed wrinkle-free.

The Potters want to know what I like for breakfast, do I need a bedtime story, how about a nightlight shaped like Snoopy? When at last they close the door, not all the way—"We'll leave a crack so we'll hear you if you have a bad dream"—I am exhausted. My head feels like it's been twisted around like a wrung-out towel. Still, I'm wide awake, amazed to discover that there are actual people like this who aren't on a weekly sitcom. I don't know what to make of The Potters, how to trust them or ask them to give me a little space. I don't know if they expect a thank-you or if they want me to be a challenge so they can add another success story to their legend. I don't even know if I like them or if they like me—we've hardly spent any time together and yet there's all this love, love, love. How can you love somebody you just met, somebody you've never asked a real question, somebody you've never had to forgive or who's never needed to forgive you?

They strike me, The Potters, as plush stuffed animals, squeezed up against you in a small closet so you can hardly breathe. I know that's not fair. I know I've got nothing to be suspicious about. I know from the talk I've heard from the kids in school who've been dumped into terrible foster homes that I should be grateful to Irene for finding me The Potters.

I lie awake, staring at the ceiling, which I can see thanks to Snoopy, and I try to picture the scene tomorrow. Everybody sitting down to the table at the same time for breakfast, which Frieda makes herself instead of just running to the 7-Eleven for a box of yesterday's doughnuts. Bill bowing his head to say grace. Ben and Brian kidding around with each other. It's like watching a science-fiction movie, except I'm the alien, the visitor from outer space who's trying to figure out human customs, and it just gets to this point where I realize that as nice as earth is, all I want is to go home to my cold, barren planet, the one with twelve moons and a dying blue sun and an exploding core.

Why? I ask myself. What's wrong with me that The Potters make me so uncomfortable? What's missing?

And then, as I cast my eyes around the room and I focus automatically on Snoopy, I suddenly know. I can hear Mom's voice at last.

"Snoopy," she says. "Give me a break. I declare a national emergency!"

Mom can always make me laugh, even when she's not around. She keeps talking.

"Who are you supposed to be in that outfit, the Bride of Frankenstein? And did you hear the joke: How many Potters does it take to screw in a lightbulb? Four! One to hold the lightbulb steady and three to turn the house around."

If there's one thing Mom isn't, it's nice-nice. She treats me like we *have* split the difference, like we're friends. She expects me to always get the joke. She's spoiled me for The Potters—or spoiled The Potters for me. Either way this isn't going to work out and the longer I let it go on the more I'm going to hurt The Potters' feelings. There's a phone in "my" room, and I search out Irene's night-or-day number, dial it.

Of course, being that it's Friday, Dad answers.

"Let me talk to Irene," I mumble in a disguised voice. I don't want to have to fight my way through him and I don't want to make his day by what I've got to say.

19

"This is Irene." She sounds out of breath and I decide not to think about why.

"It's Rayona." Before she can tip Dad off and put him on the line, I blast ahead. "I've changed my mind."

"About what?" Irene is not delighted to hear from me after her office hours.

"I'd rather be with a black family."

"Why's that, honey?" I can sense the I-knew-it smile on her face.

"See, I've never been around black people much before, and I think it would be interesting to give it a try." Let Dad explain that.

When the sun comes up, I get out of bed quietly so that I won't wake The Potters and repack my bag. Irene has promised to pick me up at seven o'clock, before she goes to work. Potty watches me with her head cocked.

"Shhhh," I warn her.

"Shhhh," she echoes in my voice.

I find a piece of stationery in the desk drawer and write The Potters a thank-you note that they'll find after I leave. I want to say something that will make them know they haven't done anything wrong.

"Dear Potter Family, Roger, and Potty," I begin, then search for the right words.

"Just one night in your lovely home has turned me into a whole new person," I go on. "I'll never forget you. I hope you don't mind but I borrowed Snoopy. It will remind me of you every time I switch him on."

I unplug Snoopy and put him with my clothes. I know beyond a doubt that The Potters will approve of my taking him. They'll be glad, sure they understand completely.

But the fact of the matter is, I can hardly wait to show Snoopy to Mom and hear what she says about him in person.

chapter three
chapter three

THERE IS NO SIGN ON Mrs. Jackson's door. She lives in an apartment off Pacific Avenue in Tacoma not all that far from a place where Mom and I once stayed for six months. Her building, I notice, has an elevator and a security system that needs to be buzzed before you can get in.

"It's Irene Baker and Rayona," Irene says into the speaker.

"Come right up," replies a woman's crisp voice, followed by the sound of the lock popping on the door.

"Mrs. Jackson is strict but she's fair," Irene informs me as the elevator climbs slowly to the third floor.

Great. She might have given me a chance to make a back-up plan while I "killed time," as she put it, at her office all morning. Dad was off delivering mail, and I had the whole place to myself because it was a Saturday.

"How strict?" I ask. "Strict about what?"

"You'll see."

The elevator door slides open. Irene leads me to 3-F and rings the bell. I hear someone at the peep-hole and it seems to me Mrs. Jackson takes her good sweet time deciding whether or not to let us in. Irene, impatient, rings the bell again.

"There's no need to burst my eardrums," an irritated voice inches away from us fusses, and we wait while an endless series of chains, poles, and dead-bolts are deactivated. It occurs to me that I haven't even had lunch.

Mrs. Jackson has dressed for the occasion of meeting me: a blue rayon dress with a navy print, medium black heels, pale stockings. She has a lace handkerchief in a pocket pushed forward by her large bosom, and her salt-and-pepper hair is arranged in an iron permanent that no little wind better try to disturb. She examines me through gold-rimmed glasses. Everything about her announces two undeniable facts: 1) church-goer, and 2) retired schoolteacher.

"So this is the unfortunate child. Let me see your hands, young lady."

I'm so unprepared for her command that I do as she asks, and she grasps my wrists firmly, looks closely at both sides of each hand. What does she expect to see?

"Good," she announces. "Not a biter."

Irene, of course, takes this opportunity to flash her own set of beauty-parlor nails while opening her briefcase. Mrs. Jackson sees, all right.

"Vanity," she states grimly, "goes before the fall."

"I thought it was pride," Irene, disappointed not to be praised, replies.

"Same thing." Mrs. Jackson is not about to be outquoted. "Look it up in the dictionary when you get home. You do *have* a dictionary."

I watch as before my eyes Irene turns into an embarrassed fourth grader.

"Yes, ma'am."

"Well, that's *something*," Mrs. Jackson reluctantly concedes.

"Here's the number where I can be reached," Irene says. "I so appreciate your willingness to handle this matter in a somewhat unorthodox fashion. The father is afraid the mother might lose custody if this went through normal channels, and I'm sure you'll agree that a girl belongs with her mama."

Mrs. Jackson is not about to agree with anything she hasn't said first. "The Lord works in unorthodox ways."

"Mysterious," Irene corrects before she can catch herself.

Mrs. Jackson's eyes blaze at the impertinence.

"There are no mysteries," she instructs Irene. "Just questions, which have not yet been solved because of human limitations or laziness."

I glance at the door and realize Mrs. Jackson sealed it back up after she let us in. No escape. The woman is still holding my wrists, and I tug slightly to release them. This draws her attention back to me.

"I am Mrs. Jackson," she tells me unnecessarily. "And you are Rayona Diane Taylor, in need of shelter and a suitable environment."

So much for having your complete existence summed up in a single sentence.

"I demand and expect honesty, punctuality, and neatness," Mrs. Jackson continues. "These qualities along with perseverance, industry, and courage will serve you well as long as you live."

Hey, I feel like clueing her. This isn't the first day of reform school. I just need, or Dad thinks I need, a place to sleep until Mom pulls herself together and saves me.

"Okay," however, is all I say.

"Okay whom?"

"Okay, Mrs. Jackson." This woman is Dad's Good Manners Fairy come to life.

"'Okay' is rather colloquial," Mrs. Jackson grades me. "But considering that this is your first day . . ."

Irene, during this interchange, has moved to stand by the door, awaiting release. Our eyes meet and I can almost hear her voice taunting, singing, "Potters, Potters, Potters."

Mrs. Jackson is heavy into rules. Where this goes, what time that happens. Going through her apartment is like a long guided tour of the most boring museum on Earth. It's as though she's thrown all her considerable energy into schedules and furniture arrangement, into imposing herself on all that surrounds her, and now the only loose thread is me, her new project.

Over the course of the afternoon, she inspects my teeth, brushes my hair, refolds my clothes before putting them in a drawer she has emptied in her second bedroom. What she doesn't do is ask me a single question or give me the opening to ask one of her. We're as distant and formal as two robots in a space station. The whole business wears us both out.

"I used to love to cook." Mrs. Jackson confesses this at four o'clock in the afternoon as if it is a flaw in her personality. To me it just sounds like good news.

"You probably aren't a big eater." Her measuring look is aimed at my stomach.

"I'm growing," I say to encourage her. I don't care what she does as long as she loves to do it, because that will take her mind off of improving me.

She sighs, not convinced. "Mr. Jackson, the Lord rest his soul, and I had five fine eaters—all grown up and moved away now—and none of them ever went hungry in our home. I'd come back from a full day at the school—I taught home ec at Lincoln High School for thirty-one years—and work magic in the kitchen. It's all about organization, Miss Taylor. Miracles can be accomplished if you make lists and will yourself to stick to them, whatever may."

"Yes, ma'am," I say, clear as if Dad has just poked me in the ribs. Mrs. Jackson shoots me an amazed glance, suspicious that I'm putting her on. I make my eyes flat and innocent, and she stares a beat longer than she has intended.

"You have possibilities, Miss Taylor," is all she will concede. "Definite possibilities."

I figured Mrs. Jackson for the liver-and-lima-beans type, maybe some healthy kind of cardboard bread, so I listen to her food stories with a lot of doubts.

Dinner, therefore, comes as a major surprise.

"I prepared too much," Mrs. Jackson says—her first admission of the possibility she could make a mistake. "I have guests so seldom these days and I'm used to cooking for an army, or for potluck church suppers."

She's not kidding. Baked ham. Coleslaw. Green beans and bacon. Mashed potatoes so light they seem like butter-flavored clouds. Pearl onions in cream sauce, plate of biscuits. A lemon meringue pie for dessert.

The food sits piled on the table between us, enough for five people, more than that.

"You think I'm a silly old fool," Mrs. Jackson says and brings her napkin to her eyes, dislodging her glasses. "It's just . . . it's just that after years of asking Miss Baker for a placement and being informed that according to regulations I'm too old, she finally called with you and I . . ." Mrs. Jackson stops, shocked at what she is about to hear herself say. "I lost control."

This woman is about to self-destruct before my eyes. I have to bail her out.

"I am so hungry," I say. "I haven't eaten all day—not since yesterday, and that was a cheese sandwich. I've never been so hungry." It seems as though there is something missing, something else I should add, and then it comes to me. "I love to eat."

Mrs. Jackson lowers her napkin slightly, regards me with bright eyes. You can almost see her balancing the equation: loves to cook equals loves to eat. We match.

"Just help yourself, Miss Taylor." Her voice has shrunk into itself, risen to a higher pitch.

"Really?" I draw the moment out.

Mrs. Jackson can only nod.

So I let loose. I'm like one of those people you see at an all-you-can-eat buffet, I stack my plate that full. There's no room for boundaries between the different items: slaw spills onto ham, beans mix with potatoes. Little white onions tuck in here and there. Two biscuits on the side.

I pick up my fork and look at Mrs. Jackson looking at me.

"What about you, Mrs. Jackson? Aren't you hungry at all?"

She seems to square her shoulders, returns her napkin to where it belongs. Her brows make a frown but she's not a bit angry.

"My dear Rayona Diane Taylor," she says, her mouth fighting with and losing to a wide, old-lady grin. "It seems like I haven't had a decent meal in twenty years."

And then she digs in, too, matches me serving for serving. We finish the potatoes first, then the creamy slaw. I get the last onion in exchange for her having the final tablespoon of beans. The one remaining biscuit, we split. She insists I take the soft top part.

"Lord, Lord, Lord," is all Mrs. Jackson can say when our plates are empty.

"I'm going to explode," I answer, but then I

remember one of her never-ever-break rules: all dishes done and put away before leaving the kitchen.

"You rest," I tell her, and scoot back my chair. "I'll clean up."

Mrs. Jackson manages to lift one arm, point a long finger at my chair.

"Nothing gets touched," she commands. "I intend to relish this devastation for hours and hours to come."

After that night, Mrs. Jackson and I are like two kids locked for the weekend in a toy store. Every rule she has previously announced, we break, shrieking at each other with laughter as we do so. We stay up late, we don't get dressed, we don't make our beds. We aren't punctual, we aren't neat. We even oversleep and miss church. We're bad influences on each other for five solid days, but when Irene calls to check up on me, Mrs. Jackson uses her policeman's voice and says that I am making slow but steady progress. What Irene doesn't know is that while Mrs. Jackson is uttering these words she is doing a wicked but very accurate imitation of Irene, swinging her hips, buffing her nails, rapidly blinking her eyes.

On Thursday evening, though, we have to get serious. Mrs. Jackson's daughter Clara has fractured her leg in a skiing accident and wants Mrs. Jackson to come and take care of her grandchildren for two months.

"Where was the accident?" I ask. I realize we've never talked about either of our families.

"Mount Rainier," Mrs. Jackson says without any expression in her voice.

"But that's right here, just south of town. You can see it on a clear day."

"Clara and her family live in Seattle," Mrs. Jackson says softly. "My one son is here in Tacoma, the other one in Portland. I have a daughter in Bellingham."

"But none of them has ever called." I speak without thinking. "In all this time."

"I generally hear from them at Christmas and on my birthday," Mrs. Jackson says, so low it's almost to herself. "They send pictures of their children and I paste them in my album."

"But . . . why?"

"You saw how I was with you that first day. That's how I raised them. They couldn't wait to get out on their own."

"But you're not really like that," I protest. "You're . . . fun."

Mrs. Jackson turns toward me, then opens her eyes wide.

"Repeat that, please."

"You're fun."

"I'm fun." Her voice is full of wonder.

"You are."

"Rayona, you are a blessing."

"When you're fun you remind me of my mom. I miss her."

"Your mother is fortunate to have a daughter who can say that. But she's not well yet, Rayona. She's in a facility, and her treatment lasts almost another three weeks."

"Irene called?"

Mrs. Jackson nods, sorry, but there's more she needs to explain to me.

"Your mother and I—the way I was with my children—are like two extremes of love. I strove to be everything, and I was no fun. She's all fun, but I worry she doesn't try hard enough to be there for you."

"The two of you need to split the difference," I say, Mom's words coming out of my mouth.

"Mr. Jackson had his moments," Mrs. Jackson goes on, exploring her memories. "But he could never hold a steady job and so that task fell to me. I made a success of myself and . . . Well, let's just say I let him know it. The children loved him better than me, and he let me know that. We both felt cheated, both felt things weren't fair."

"But look how you cooked for them all," I rise to

her defense, recalling my first night at her apartment.

"I gave them food in a way that they couldn't enjoy it." Mrs. Jackson's still thinking back, understanding things she hasn't understood before. "I demanded gratitude, and that stood in the way of pleasure."

"It's not too late," I try to perk her up. "You can surprise Clara."

"How?" She wants to believe me.

"Be fun."

"Do you think?"

"Once you've started something like being fun, you can't stop."

"If only . . ." Mrs. Jackson looks hopeful, almost eager, then her expression clouds. "But what will happen to you, Rayona?"

I swallow. I don't want to lose her, but she has a lot of time to make up for and not much time to do it. I tell myself I'm not her problem. I tell myself she and Clara are overdue for a national holiday together. I tell myself I wouldn't want anybody to stand between me and Mom when she's ready to come home.

"Let Dad figure it out." I try to imagine this happening: Dad's face screwed up in thought, coming up with a plan. It doesn't work. He keeps opening his eyes, looking at something behind me or off to the side. But this time I won't let him do it. I am

33

his problem, that's the deal.

"I don't believe he and Irene are seeing each other anymore," Mrs. Jackson says. "I understand they've had a . . . falling out."

At least that means no Potters, I think to myself, but aloud I say, "Then I can be with him till Mom's released. He *is* my father. It's just a few weeks. We can stand each other for that long."

chapter four
chapter four

WELL, I'M WRONG. I DON'T fit into Dad's life, unless somehow I bring Mom along with me. When I realize this, I'm too scared to get mad at him.

"Don't blame me, baby." Dad senses how worried I am and is full of apology when he picks me up at Mrs. Jackson's. It's so early that it's still dark outside. My suitcase is packed, my clothes spotless and neatly folded. "I'm in a one-room studio, away at work from four in the morning till three in the afternoon. That's no way for a little girl to live."

I've already said my good-byes to Mrs. Jackson. Not so much good-byes as see-you-soons, which makes them easier. She's dressed, ready for her own trip to Clara, and studies Dad carefully, as if remembering every word so that she can quote it back to him if he doesn't do right by me. He's glad when we leave the apartment and it's just the two of us in the taxi he's left waiting downstairs.

"We could visit at night."

"At night I'm so tired I fall asleep with my eyes open."

I wonder whether that has something to do with why Dad and Irene fell out.

"But I had an inspiration," Dad says all phony cheerful. "It's a win-all-around proposition. You'll visit your grandmother for a month. Get to know her."

"Aunt Ida?" That's what Mom calls her mother, who lives back on the reservation in Montana. I've met her a couple of times, and she hasn't exactly struck me as a person who would be glad to have me dumped on her doorstep, especially by Dad, whom she's never liked or even met.

"No, no." Dad is as horrified by the idea of Aunt Ida as I am. "Your *other* grandma. My mother. She'll love you to pieces."

His mother? Dad mentions his family so seldom and then so vaguely that I have all but forgotten he has one. I get cards, sometimes wrapped presents, clothes in the wrong sizes—from his mother, his aunt, and his grandmother—but they live far away back east somewhere. I've heard their voices on the phone once or twice but I've never laid eyes on them.

"Is she coming here?" I ask hopefully but fearing the worst.

"Better." Dad says, "You're going there, on an airplane! And I'm going to take you! This minute!"

Something about the way he sounds makes me ask: "Do they know?"

"Not yet!" Every sentence Dad says has an exclamation point behind it. "It's a surprise! I'll call them and let them know when we pass through Chicago!"

I love being a surprise. I really do. I love it almost as much as getting a booster shot, as having a cavity filled, as the first day at a new school in the middle of the year.

"Shouldn't I at least say good-bye to Mom before I leave?" I ask Dad. She and I have never before been in different states at the same time, and the thought bothers me.

"They say she should have quiet," Dad answers. "No upsets or outside influences. Just concentrate on getting well."

"I wouldn't upset her."

"You would, baby, without meaning to. She'd feel guilty. You can come back as soon as she's ready."

Dad is so unhelpful about Mom that I don't tell him my worries about flying on an airplane, or my nervousness about what to expect when we get to wherever we're heading. Instead, I just go along with what he tells me, act as if everything strange is normal. I convince him because he isn't paying that much attention. I convince him because he wants to be convinced. But I don't convince myself.

The plane seems enormous—full of strangers who know what they are doing, who don't feel it necessary to listen to every word the stewardess tells us about buckling our seat belts and breathing from oxygen masks that in an emergency will fall from the ceiling, about how if we crash over water we each have personal life jackets tucked under our seats. They look hard to put on. I read all the instructions on the card in the pocket of the seat in front of me, memorize them because there'll be no time for review if the engine fails. I locate the nearest exit, am discouraged by the size of the people who'll have to get out of it before me.

In the midst of all this I think of Mom, safe on the ground in some hospital, protected from feeling guilty about me, and something truly frightening happens. I stop liking her. It's a feeling like holding your breath—all tight and uncomfortable, motionless. The words "This is her fault" seal my lips and I shut my ears against all her familiar excuses for herself. For just that moment I'm inside the small room of my own self and all the doors are locked, the windows covered with curtains, the lights off.

"I don't like you," I say to Mom in my head.

And then her voice answers, plain and clear as if she is actually speaking.

"*You* don't like me. *I* don't like me. Stand in line to join the club."

That's Mom's secret: nobody can like her less than she likes herself down deep, so you wind up liking her more than she does by default.

The moment passes, The door opens, the curtains part, the light comes on. My feelings for Mom are not about liking or not liking. They just are.

Dad insists I sit by the window so I can watch the takeoff. The problem is, I look out and am sure the wing is on fire and nobody else notices. What do I do? Sound the alarm and risk being embarrassed by being wrong, or crash without having to blush? I think about this long enough for the answer not to matter because suddenly we're racing along the runway and then—pow—we're off the ground, climbing into the sky, leaning to the side so that all of Seattle, Tacoma, and the mountain is contained by the little square window next to me. Everything, everyone I've ever known fixed there in a space smaller than a TV screen.

Dad does one of those things he does every once in a while that blots out all of the times he's disappointed me: he kisses me on the cheek, just like that.

"It's an adventure, baby. Enjoy it. Learn to take

your adventures where you find them."

I turn to him. His green eyes are cool and calm in his dark, handsome face. He's mine, I think, and I've got him next to me for at least eight hours. There's no adventure bigger than that, and I follow his advice, I take it where I can find it. I find his hand with mine, work my fingers between his. Entwined, the tan of my skin against the coffee of his reminds me of that bracelet of three twisted metals—copper, bronze, and steel—he always wears for luck. We don't speak because there's nothing that needs saying, but even when we're served our meal of chicken and potatoes, a hard roll and a piece of orange cake, we each awkwardly eat with our free hand. We don't let go of each other all the way to Chicago.

So here I stand in the airport, waiting for the flight to Louisville, witness to another of Dad's end of a complicated pay-telephone conversation.

"Mother!"

He's back to his exclamation points.

"No, everything is fine." Pause. He turns to me. "She's going to tell her sister, my aunt Edna, to get on the extension phone." Pause. "You'll never guess. No. No."

They're guessing.

"No. Wait, I'll tell you: Chicago, Illinois!"

I can actually hear two women's voices pop out of the receiver as Dad holds it away from his ear in anticipation.

"Chicago, *Illinois*!" they shout.

"Wait," Dad says, putting the phone against his face. "I'm not alone." Quickly he pulls it away again and I hear a chorus that contains the word *"Christine."*

"Not this time," Dad says. "Better!"

Now he really distances himself and out of the little black holes blasts my name: *"Rayona!"*

"You guessed it," Dad says. And before they can react, he goes on. "We'll be there in an hour and a half. I thought it was long overdue for a visit."

This time Dad actually puts the receiver between us so I can listen more easily. The women are talking like a washing machine, their voices swishing and chugging with questions and arrangements. They're talking as much to each other as they're speaking to Dad. It's as though they've turned into one of those science experiments you see on TV where someone pours an odd-colored liquid into a test tube and suddenly smoke starts pouring out.

"Well," Dad interrupts, "we'd better go now or we'll miss our flight." Pause. "Four thirty-eight. United from Chicago." Pause. "Mother, you don't have to . . ." Pause. "Okay, great, wonderful. We'll see you there." Pause. "Of course she knows, don't be silly." Pause. "I love you, too." Pause. "We will." Pause. "Bye, Mother; bye, Aunt Edna."

When Dad hangs up, he looks beat. "You want something to eat?" he asks me. "Some gum? A comic book?"

I say yes and we go to the concession stand. After Dad has paid and we're walking toward our gate I can't stand it anymore, so I ask the question that's been burning a hole in my pocket.

"Of course I know *what*?"

Dad sighs, looks at me, tries to think how to not tell me whatever it is I already know. Can't think of a way.

"Well, it's like this," he starts, sighs again. "My mother, my aunt, my grandmother?"

I nod. I know who we're going to see.

"The thing is," Dad goes on. "They're white."

It's a short flight to Louisville, too short to have your whole life history revised in a voice shouted over the drone of an engine. I listen, chewing a piece of Juicy Fruit until all its flavor is gone, then sticking the wad in an ashtray and popping another into my mouth.

"My father—your grandfather—was black, naturally," Dad tells me. "And before World War II he and my mother, who isn't, fell in love with each other and got married."

Even I can tell that this is a pretty short version of a long story.

"They moved to California and had me," he continues, "and then he was . . ." Dad looks at the airplane ceiling, at all the little buttons that control the air conditioning and summon the stewardess and turn on the reading light. "Died," he says.

He's leaving something out, some detail, some secret within a secret, but I am so anxious to find out what happened next, to get to the "me" part, that I let it go by.

"I don't remember him at all," Dad continues. "So my mother—your grandmother—came back to Kentucky to live with her sister and mother and that's where I grew up until I joined the army myself."

I have learned more about Dad's past in the last two minutes than in all the years of my life so far and am speechless with questions. The original one finally comes out first.

"*White?*"

"Irish, actually."

I do something in my mind that's like arithmetic, like adding up numbers and then dividing them to get an average.

"That means I'm *Irish?*"

"Plus a lot of other things. Indian on your mom's side, and black from your grandfather's."

43

It doesn't register. I think of shamrocks and don't feel anything special. How can I be Irish?

"Do they know I don't know I'm Irish?" I ask Dad, meaning this mystery family I'm about to meet.

"Baby, let me tell you. To them you *are*." He reaches into his back pocket, pulls out his wallet, opens the flap that conceals the secret compartment, and digs out a crinkly-edged photograph. "Here," he says and passes it to me.

I stare at three women. One older and stern looking. One tall and smiling in a way that makes me think she doesn't do it all that often. And one pretty, all dressed up, with makeup on.

"Which one's my grandmother?" I ask Dad, and he points to the pretty one.

"Her name's Marcella," he informs me. "Marcella Taylor, same last name as ours. She can come on a little strong but she's been begging me to bring you to meet her for years."

Then why didn't you? I want to ask, but then a more important question occurs to me.

"Does Mom know we're Irish?"

Dad actually squirms in his seat—there's no other way to describe it. It's as though he's being screwed into the upholstery. "We need to talk about that part," he says.

I wait. Right now I have nothing to contribute to the conversation we're about to have.

"No," Dad whispers.

"No?"

"No, she doesn't know," Dad goes on. He's hunched down so our eyes are on the same level. "I didn't tell her when we first met and then . . . I never got around to it. There were so many other . . . stuff. I mean, it was enough, me being black." He looks at me, helpless, begging me with his mint-flavored eyes to agree.

"Like, she has no *idea*?" It knocks me out that I know something Mom doesn't even suspect.

Dad shakes his head. "I mean, you could tell her. You'll probably want to, after all."

I can tell he hopes I won't. I put this idea in the bank to let it draw compound interest, a concept from my math book that I don't quite understand.

"Or it could be kind of a secret, just between us," Dad offers.

Then he takes a big risk: he tells me the truth. "I'd really appreciate that," he says.

My brain is full of blowing snow, the screen of a TV when you wake up in the middle of the night after leaving it on. "The Star-Spangled Banner" is over. Even the test pattern has shut off. Dad has never actually asked anything from me before, and the asking feels like a gift wrapped up in tissue paper.

"Are you ashamed of being Irish?" I ask him

while I think about what I'm going to do.

"No," Dad insists. "No. It's just . . . you don't want to give every part of you away so it can be used against you, you know what I mean?"

I don't, but I try to act as if I do.

"Secrets are big in my—our—family, Ray. They're like vitamin pills."

I have no idea what he's talking about, but I think of that other secret, the secret secret, that he hasn't told me yet. I sense I have to earn the right to that one by keeping this one, and at the same time I begin to see an advantage for myself to secrets. Having a secret with somebody means they trust you, because you could always betray them, you could always tell. When you know somebody's secret, it's up to you to protect them. They need you. They can't afford to take you for granted any-more.

I like it that Dad doesn't know yet that he can count on me. I like it that he has to be very careful.

We've run out of time: the plane is making its descent for landing. I fasten my seat belt, chew the last of my gum to keep my ears from plugging up. I want to be at the top of my hearing capacity when I get off this plane. I don't want to miss another word for the rest of my life.

chapter five
chapter five

I CAN'T SEE OVER THE people in front of us in line but, being tall, Dad can and all of a sudden his hands are around my waist and he's hoisting me up, raising me above everyone else. "There she is," he tells me.

I search the crowd of people waiting, but my grandmother sees me first. When my eyes get to her she's already smiling, pointing with one hand to a giant Raggedy Ann doll she's holding in the other. She's dressed in a red short-sleeved blouse with a bow at the neck and a white skirt. She has curly brown hair and rhinestone earrings. Aunt Ida, my other grandma, is like a fruitcake, dense and heavy, but this woman is more like a vanilla Hostess cupcake, the kind with the little curlicue of icing over the top and a cream center. She can't take her eyes off me and doesn't look a bit surprised at what I look like. Dad must have sent pictures. Suddenly I realize her eyes are the exact same shade of green as Dad's. He's not making all this up.

Dad can't wave because his hands are full of me. He sets me back on my feet.

"Run to her, give her a kiss," he tells me. "It would make her so happy."

Making people happy is not something I've had a guaranteed chance to do all that often, so I think, Why not? I hand Dad my gum, take a breath, and break through the crowd in her direction. She meets me halfway, carrying Raggedy Ann before her as if the doll is what I must really be interested in, not her. But when we meet, I duck under Raggedy and dive directly into the woman's soft, pale, talcum-smelling arms. She whirls me around, squeezes me tight against her breasts and, like nearly everyone else I've ever met for the first time, gets my name wrong.

"Ramona," she whispers in my ear in a southern accent, "I'm so glad to finally meet you."

Then Dad's there, too, his big arms around us both, his cologne mixing with my grandmother's perfume. "Mother," he says in a voice with no phony exclamation points, "you look great. I don't know how to thank you."

"Thank *me*?" My grandmother's voice is muffled against her son's chest. "I'm the one to thank you for bringing this precious doll baby."

It occurs to me, squashed between them, that the

three of us must make a strange sight to other people in the airport. They might try to figure us out but they'd never guess the truth in a million years.

Finally we break apart and somehow my grandmother has managed it that I'm holding Raggedy Ann in my arms.

"Let's get ourselves over to the baggage claim and hurry on home," my grandmother says. "Edna must be chomping at the bit and your grandmother"—she nods to Dad—"has dinner timed to the second. Woe betide us if her sweet potatoes get cold."

I don't know what exactly is in store but I do know one thing. I'll never again be able to look out a small window and see my whole world from it, not unless I'm in a spaceship heading for the moon.

I ride in the back seat of my grandmother's yellow Mercury—because of Dad's long legs, he gets the front, it is explained—and don't talk on the drive from the airport. Compared to downtown Seattle or Tacoma, Louisville seems like one big park—all flowers, trees, and sweet smells. The scenery is gentler, the air heavier, the sounds as muted as the bump of a tied-up ship against a wooden dock.

My grandmother points out the sights as we go along, each announcement followed by "Remember, Elgin?" as if she's trying to draw Dad back into his childhood.

"Um-hum," he answers each time, or "Oh, yeah."

"It's lovely to have you both home," my grandmother says. "I just hope you're planning a long visit."

When this gets no "Um-hum" or "Oh, yeah" from Dad, my grandmother glances at him, waits, and finally asks, "Elgin?"

"Actually, Mother, I've got to go right back. Tomorrow. I'm using up my sick days at the post office as it is."

I can feel her disappointment, clear as if the car has begun to go over a rough stretch of highway, but to my surprise she doesn't say anything.

"Ray, though," Dad hurries on, "she can stay for two or three weeks. Then I was kind of hoping you and Aunt Edna could put her on a flight and I'd meet her in Seattle."

"That little child, travel all alone?" My grandmother's shock is an umbrella she opens to cover her sorrow that Dad is leaving so soon. "I won't hear of it. If it comes to that, Edna and I will just chauffeur her out there ourselves."

We all try to think about that. For my part it is beyond imagination.

"It's more than four thousand miles round-trip," Dad points out.

"We haven't had a vacation in years," my grandmother answers. "Besides, then maybe at least we'll get to meet Christine, my daughter-in-law."

The mention of Mom's name sends us all to our own secret places. Then Mom will know! I think. I try to picture this woman in a red bow dealing with Mom—and the funny thing is, it's not so hard to do. They're different enough that they might hit it off. But then there would be nothing just between Dad and me.

A golden porch light is on at the house where my grandmother stops the car, and before we even open our doors, a large woman comes running down the steps, down the walk, and practically drags Dad out of the car.

"I'm going to kill you, Elgin," she threatens, hugging him for all she's worth. "It's unforgivable how you don't keep in touch." This in between kissing him hard on each cheek, each eyelid, and his forehead.

"Hey, Aunt Edna." Dad is smiling, hugging her back. "You shrunk."

"Of course I shrunk," she says. "That's what old people neglected by their loved ones do." She stands back at last, looks him over. "You need a haircut."

"Meet your grand-niece," Dad tells her, and beckons me out of the car.

She studies me. "I can see your father in you," she says at last, and shakes my hand like a man. Somehow that puts me more at ease. I have the feeling that with this Aunt Edna you've got to earn the hugs—and the right to hug.

"Mama's inside," she announces to all of us, and I notice that both my grandmother and my dad respond by moving faster. "Mama," who is actually my newfound great-grandmother, is standing in the doorway. Her gray hair is done up in a bun, and she's heavy-set with thin, long fingers, which she taps against each other non-stop as if she's sending a Morse code message. Her body is stiff, rigid, until Dad touches the top of her head with his lips and says, "Hiya, Grandma." Then she sags so hard he almost has to catch her.

"I never thought I'd live . . ." she begins.

"I'm sorry," Dad says—a word that seems to show up more and more in his vocabulary. "I'm sorry. I'm sorry."

The four of them have a history that happened long before I was born and the only thing I can tell about it for sure is that it must have been intense.

"He's got to leave right away," my grandmother gets the bad news over with. "But the little one is ours for weeks and weeks."

This makes my great-grandmother look stricken. Then, still with the same betrayed expression, she turns to me.

"Hey," I say.

"Isn't she the most adorable thing you ever saw?" my grandmother demands more than asks.

"Isn't she our Elgin all over?" Aunt Edna chimes in. It's clear that they're pushing hard for their mother to approve of me.

"Call me Mamaw," Mama insists, then demands, "What's that you have in your hands?"

I look. I'm still clutching Raggedy Ann and I hold the doll up to show her. Everyone seems to catch their breath.

"I'll bet she's tired from her long trip," Mamaw finally decides, and nobody is about to tell her that my grandmother just gave her to me in the airport.

"Yes, ma'am," I say, and Dad lobs me a glance of pure one hundred percent gratitude.

Mamaw gives a grim smile in my direction. "Good upbringing," she nods. "You're a fine young lady. I'll bet you're just as tired as your Raggedy. How about a bread-and-butter-and-jelly sandwich before bedtime?"

"What kind of jelly?" I ask. I sense Dad's silent prayer and throw in, "Ma'am."

I have passed Mamaw's final test.

"Tell your Mamaw what's your favorite," she says to me. "And if we don't have some in the larder, your aunt Edna will run to the store and fetch it."

It's grape, they've got it, and at last we all go into the house.

chapter six
chapter six

OKAY, I'M NOT EXACTLY A stranger to being a stranger. All my life I've been the new kid in school, the new tenant in the apartment house, and lately the illegal foster child in two under-the-counter placements. What's weird to me is being a stranger in a place that everybody insists is home—mine, by right of being Dad's daughter. When my grandmother, Aunt Edna, and Mamaw tell me, "Here's your chair," they mean it: *my* chair. When they say, "Here's your great-great-grandmother from Ireland's table," they really mean *my* great-great-grandmother from Ireland. When they say, "Here's a picture of your father when he was your age, sitting on the back steps," they mean my father, *here,* on the very steps on which I at any moment am also free to sit.

All this my-ness is like that phenomenon I've heard of, déjà vu, where it feels as though a thing has happened to you once before. Except it doesn't seem that way to me, it just seems that it *should* have because they're so convincing.

"My" family, I can tell you, are neither as pushy as The Potters nor as ready to play as Mrs. Jackson. They are . . . real-life people—cranky with each other one minute and then behaving as if nothing happened the next. After the first few minutes they act as though I've always been around, as if I am aware where everything is kept and how everything's done. They don't get mad when I make a mistake, like not knowing where they put the clean glasses or how to turn on the bathroom light, they just seem mildly puzzled.

It's after I go to bed in Dad's old room and they think I'm asleep that I hear an edge line their voices.

"What time is your flight?" my grandmother asks Dad. It must be ten o'clock.

"Seven-thirty."

There's a pause, then Aunt Edna says, "You can borrow my car when you go to see *her*." The way she says *her* wakes me up completely. "I called her as soon as we heard from you. Naturally she'll be expecting at least a hello-good-bye."

"You didn't have to do that," Dad says. He sounds somewhere between put out and grateful.

"You certainly didn't, Edna," Mamaw says. "Elgin brought that child to *us*."

"She's family, too, Mama." Aunt Edna's not a bit sorry for whatever she's done. "*She* loves him just like we do. She'd be crushed if he left without seeing her. She hasn't been all that well."

I have the impression Aunt Edna's said this last part especially to Dad.

"What do you mean?" he asks, as my great-grandmother demands, "You *don't* keep in touch with her, Edna?"

"Of course I do. Why wouldn't I? I'm the one who took Elgin to see her every weekend of his childhood. I saw how she hated to see him leave. She's got tender feelings."

"It's her fault he left in the first place," my grandmother declares. "She talked him into it."

"It's true," Mamaw agrees. "If it wasn't for her, he would never have joined the army."

They're speaking of Dad as if he isn't in the room, and I'm caught up in the mystery of this "her."

"You know it was time," Dad says. "I couldn't stay here after I was grown."

"Well, she pushed you, at least admit that." My grandmother, for all her gushiness to me and Dad at the airport, is not about to be appeased on this subject.

"Just go and come back before it's too late," Aunt Edna says, and I hear a set of keys jingling.

"We'll wait up and have Stork Club before bed, just like old times."

"I made my pineapple upside-down cake," Mamaw reports. "Thank the good Lord I had the ingredients because you certainly didn't give me a chance to shop."

"I'll be back in an hour," Dad says, and before anyone can object I hear the front door open and shut.

There's silence and I imagine the three women sitting where they were, staring daggers at each other. The suspense is driving me crazy, so I get out of bed, tiptoe down the stairs to the dark dining room, and wearing a pair of Dad's old pajamas, some seersucker material printed with sailboats, I walk into the light of the living-room doorway.

"Who is *she*?" I ask, and watch each of their faces change from stone to something else: my grandmother looks sorry that I've overheard the conversation; Aunt Edna looks as though she approves of my eavesdropping; and my great-grandmother looks surprised to see me at all, as though she's forgotten who I am—but then she explains her reaction: "Child, in that outfit I thought you were my sugarplum come back to life, just like he used to be. Come give your Mamaw a kiss and then help me set the table. You haven't *lived* until you've tasted my upside-down."

While we work to lay out plates and forks, I

notice all three of them watching the wall clock. Dad said an hour and an alarm is going off in exactly sixty minutes.

"Her?" I ask again, not knowing what else to call the mysterious stranger.

"Technically, she's your second cousin," my grandmother says. "My late husband, Earl—your grandfather—was her first cousin. By an odd coincidence she and I share the same first name."

"'Marcella,'" Mamaw reminds us.

"A *nice* woman," Aunt Edna assures me. "She owned a grocery store but is now retired."

There is some detail they're leaving out. The sight of my hand against the white tablecloth reminds me what it must be.

"And she's black," I say more than ask.

They seem slightly embarrassed at this deduction, but my impression is that it's more because they've been reluctant to say so than because they don't like black people. After all, they seem crazy about Dad and me.

They nod at the same time, as if all three of their heads are attached to one puppet string.

"So do I get to meet her, too, while I'm visiting?"

"Certainly," Aunt Edna promises.

"If you really want to," my grandmother says.

"If we can find the time, what with everything else," Mamaw worries.

"Good," I say. Suddenly, after being so alone—
just Mom and me—it seems as though I'm getting a
new relative every five minutes. As far as I'm concerned, there can't be too many. Every one of them
is an additional barrier between me and The Potters,
or being all alone. I think of Irene, of her question,
her ploy as a way to get at Dad. "Black or white?"
she had asked me. Little did she suspect I was so rich
that the only right answer was "Both!"

chapter seven
chapter seven

I SETTLE IN AS IF I'm staying for a year, as if there is no Mom getting better, no Dad who, according to my grandmother—who's told me six times—kissed me good-bye on the forehead while I was still asleep and left for Seattle without ever finishing his story. No life waiting for me that's loaded with question marks and changes.

Here it's all routine. Cornflakes, orange juice from concentrate for breakfast, a peanut-butter-and-banana-sandwich for lunch, and a big balanced-diet type meal at five-thirty every night, followed by a recitation of the Rosary and two and one half hours in front of the TV in the living room. We watch an endless mixture of comedies and westerns, and the television is our window through which to spy on other worlds—each of which has all its major and minor problems solved within either thirty or sixty minutes, commercials included.

On Saturday afternoons we do projects. Aunt Edna, who works at an office all week, buys a kit with which you can make statues. You mix plaster of Paris, pour it into one of the red plastic molds provided: George Washington, an Indian chief with a feather headdress, a little mermaid sitting on a rock, a cocker spaniel dog. We fill the molds, make sure there are no hidden bubbles, and set them upside down to harden over night. On Sunday we pop them free, and if we have been careful, there are these perfect casts, ready for us to decorate with any colors we like.

We do a lot of art. Aunt Edna fancies herself an artist and has whole boxes of paint-by-number blank canvases that, once we match the right color with the right number, will turn into forest glens, the Mona Lisa, and Pocahontas saving Captain John Smith's life. I am not stupid. I realize that all these Indian scenes and projects—Aunt Edna's bought a beadwork loom as well, but we never get around to it—are intended to make me proud of my heritage. We never say this out loud—that would be bad taste, I think she thinks—but I appreciate her good intentions. Sunday nights Aunt Edna and I play Monopoly and I take it as a compliment that she tries hard to win. She doesn't give an inch, doesn't let me take back a bad move. "Let it be a lesson for your life," she advises me. "This time it's just a game, later . . ." she trails off, as if someday I'm going to be faced with the real choice of mortgaging Park Place in order to buy New York Avenue. I mind it that there's no squares on the board for Montana and Washington, but in their absence Aunt Edna and I both try to be the first one to land on the red rectangle of Kentucky, as if it gives us a solid home base and an advantage.

I am my grandmother's responsibility during weekdays since she doesn't have a job "outside the home." She takes me to see Churchill Downs, where the Kentucky Derby is run, takes me to Frisch's Big Boy drive-in for a secret fish sandwich ("Don't tell Mamaw. She'll claim I ruined your appetite for the nice supper she's making."), takes me to Penney's and buys me new clothes, because she doesn't have time to sew them from scratch herself, since it's too hot in Louisville for what I've brought from Seattle.

If she notices the looks we get from some of the salesladies and waitresses, looks that ask what a normal-looking white lady like my grandmother is doing with a different-colored kid like me, she never once lets on. She must have gotten practiced with this habit when Dad was growing up, I figure, because she's so natural about it. After the first few days I follow her lead—I don't pay any attention either, but I always make a big deal about calling her Grandma when someone stares too long. It makes them glance away fast.

Mamaw is determined to teach me how to cook, and we spend hours in the kitchen, whispering, because she has refused to show my grandmother and great-aunt how to make anything but fried chicken. ("In case I ever get sick," my great-grandmother explains, "I don't want to starve.")

From me, though, no recipe is sacred, not even the famous pineapple upside-down cake. "It's your legacy," she tells me. "You're my only great-grandchild and this knowledge must not be lost to the world."

We make whipped boiled sweet potatoes with molasses, brown sugar, and cream, form them into balls by cupping them in our hands, stick a marshmallow in the center, then roll them in crushed cornflake crumbs. She watches me mix pie dough, flatten it with a long tube of a glass vase dusted with flour, then, when it's round and wide enough, she helps me wrap it around and around the vase before unfurling it on a pie tin and fluting the edges with a fork.

Mamaw passes along everything she thinks is worth my knowing how to do, but she doesn't approve one night after the Rosary—a baseball game on TV has replaced our regular programs so we have the evening free—when my grandmother sits in a rocking chair, pats her lap for me to sit in it, and says, "Now I'm going to teach you a special song."

I've got to explain something about lap sitting. I never remember having done it before and the very idea makes me uncomfortable. Mom is not a "toucher," as she calls people who specialize in hugging and kissing, and though The Potters and, eventually, Mrs. Jackson would have loved for me to cuddle up with them, it always seemed kind of disloyal to Mom's opinions to do it, so I resisted.

There's no denying my grandmother though, not after we have the conspiracy of the fish sandwiches between us, so I climb on and sit stiffly until she rocks back, pulls me into her, and begins to hum in my ear a kind of dancy melody.

"Oh I don't know how and I don't know when," she sings, then apparently forgets the words and so substitutes, *"da DA da Rosie Mannion."*

"Saints preserve us," Mamaw shouts from the kitchen where she's washing dishes. "Let that woman rest in peace."

But my grandmother pays no attention. Back and forth we go, me resisting, her refusing to be resisted, as she half-sopranos, half-hums verse after verse. Aunt Edna, across from us, taps her foot.

"That was your great-great-grandmother's own song," she informs me when my grandmother finally pauses for breath. "A man wrote it just for her before she even left Ireland. At the time she was only seven years older than you are now."

This news stuns me so much that I actually do lean back into my grandmother's chest, and the suddenness of our combined weight almost tips over the chair.

"She was quite a character," Aunt Edna goes on. "She brought the table"—she points to a round table covered with photographs of Dad at every age—"clear over on the boat. In steerage, yet. And that," she nods at a glass dish on the mantel, "was hers, too. She's everywhere in this room, though she's dead and gone . . ." She takes a moment to calculate.

"Thirty-four blessed years, God rest her soul," Mamaw, not missing a word, shouts from the kitchen. From her tone I can tell they weren't exactly fond of each other.

My grandmother repeats the verses of the song so many times that it sticks in my brain, like the McDonald's jingle. The music is mixed with a whole set of other impressions: my grandmother's soft firmness, Aunt Edna's unyielding opinions, Mamaw's eagle ears in the next room. And all of that is jumbled up with the warm, humid Southern summer night, the surprise of being not just with, but actually in, a family of strong white women who never seem to disappear without saying good-bye, who have laps and recipes and rituals like the Rosary that they follow without fail every night, who seem to prefer being with me in this room to being anywhere else on earth. It's overwhelming, this banquet of impressions, and just before I drift off to sleep from the sheer exhaustion of it all, from the steady, sure rock of my grandmother's chair and the monotonous chant that seems to last forever, I ask, "Was Rose my great-great-grandmother's name?"

I know they answer. I can almost hear the words through layers of quilts and pillows, but I can't be sure of them later, and the chance to question them again never seems to arise.

chapter eight
chapter eight

ONE NIGHT, DURING MY SECOND week in Louisville, in the middle of a rerun of the *Mary Tyler Moore Show*, there's a knock on the back door. Just one knock, but unignorable in its insistence.

Mamaw, Aunt Edna, and my grandmother exchange looks.

"Yes, it is, and I don't for a minute apologize," Aunt Edna tells them, and gets up to answer. "I thought it better here than there. Rayona has had enough dislocation for one brief lifetime."

Mamaw and my grandmother have swung into rapid cleaning actions, straightening and patting couch pillows, adjusting lampshades, smoothing their dresses, although they and the house are already perfectly neat.

"Turn off that dang TV," Mamaw orders my grandmother. It's the first time I've heard any of them say something approaching a cuss word.

"Come in, come in. It's good of you to drop by," Aunt Edna is saying from the rear of the house. "You should have used the front door. You're most welcome. It's been too long."

She must be nervous, I think. She never talks this much in one stretch.

Mamaw and my grandmother stand up in front of their chairs as if ready for military inspection. Though I don't know what's going on, I stand up, too, just as a small, plump, elderly black woman walks timidly into the room—timidly until she sees me, and then there's no stopping her. She races across the floor on feet as small and nimble as a cartoon lady and doesn't stop until she's buried my head between her breasts so deeply I can hear the pound of her heart.

"Sweet Jesus." The voice comes from so far inside her that it almost seems to be my own self talking. "Now I can die a happy woman."

I am continually amazed at the reaction to me of people I keep meeting in Louisville. If they are this fond of me, where have they been all my life when I needed somebody to tell me I was . . . important? No sooner do I ask myself that question than I know the answer—though I don't exactly understand it. Dad. For his own reasons, he was so completely secretive about his side of the family that I finally lost interest, finally believed he didn't have any living blood relatives except for me. But now, out of the blue, here is this army of women, all ages, two colors, revolving around me as if I am their dreams come true.

Finally, "Cousin Marcella," who this clearly must be, releases me and I draw in a big breath to keep myself from fainting for lack of oxygen. She doesn't completely let me go—she puts me at arm's length and scans me up and down.

"Look at that hair," she says to no one in particular. "Look at that nose! Look at those lips! But what happened to your daddy's green eyes?"

She makes me feel as though I have accidentally misplaced Dad's eyes and substituted for them in my head with dark brown.

"I have my mom's eyes," I hear myself say, though I have never thought such a thing before. And of course the minute I mention her name I am overcome with missing Mom, missing the way she smells, the sound of her singing in the shower. The sound of her night breathing.

The entire room reads my mind.

"She misses her mama!" Cousin Marcella shouts.

"Of course you do, honey." My grandmother reassures me that this emotion is entirely natural.

Except that no sooner am I told that I miss Mom, in someone else's voice than my brain's, out loud, than a whole different set of feelings crowd into my head. I do *not* miss Mom's disappointing me, I want to yell. I don't miss Mom not showing up when she promises to. I don't miss Mom disappearing into her other life without even holding on to my hand. I yearn for one of these nice women to say that they feel sorry for me, that I'm amazing for not complaining about all that's happened. I want people to stop pretending that everything's okay, to stop ignoring how crazy it is. I want somebody to accuse Mom of being what she is: a rotten mother.

No I don't. If anybody bad-mouthed Mom, I realize, I'd go off like one of those paper birthday-party favors that pop when you pull at both ends. I'd say you had to know Mom to understand her, that, like she always insists, you had to walk a mile in her moccasins to feel all the sharp, pointy rocks in her private road through your thin soles. I'd lie and claim Mom and I had talked all this over before she left and that I was in complete agreement with whatever she thought was good for her, for us. I'd have no choice but to be on Mom's side, so I'm relieved that not a word of criticism passes the lips of these polite, don't-rock-the-boat relatives.

"I know she'll be well soon." Aunt Edna gives me one of her spooky I've-got-your-number-and-it's-okay-with-me looks. "I was really sick myself one time—twice—and here I am, healthy as a race-horse."

"Edna, don't worry the child with *that* old news," Mamaw cuts in. "She just wants human sympathy."

They're all holding their arms out for me, one way or another, and I feel pulled in four directions. Which woman will win the prize of consoling me and therefore shame the others? I have a sense that whichever one I go to, the other three will never feel quite the same about me again, so I chicken out, I place them back where they all want to be.

"I've got Dad's long legs." I announce, as if no part of me is actually mine.

"You do!" they exclaim in such a chorus that for a terrible moment I'm reminded of The Potters.

"And you've got a brain in your head," Aunt Edna, who has seen right through me, observes.

Cousin Marcella sits down and Mamaw leaves. At first I think she's being rude and I cringe with embarrassment, but no, she instantly reappears having somehow put together a plate of cookies and a tinkling pitcher of iced tea with lemon slices floating in it. These women can move fast when they need to.

"Don't ruin your appetite," my grandmother warns Marcella, "because you *have* to stay for dinner."

Marcella glances at her as if to judge how serious she is—and is satisfied that the invitation is genuine.

71

Instinctively I know that my grandmother doesn't fool around with matters of hospitality. That's probably where Dad got his habit of always insisting I "ma'am" and "sir" every grown-up in earshot.

"Meatloaf," Aunt Edna adds encouragingly.

But now that Marcella knows she won't upset anyone by staying, she's free to go.

"You all are kindness personified," she says, "but I'd best beat the traffic. I just wanted to get over here to meet this beauty before she ran out on me."

Why do I feel guilty? Nobody's mentioned me going anywhere.

"I'd invite you home," she says to me, and shakes her head "no" at the same time. "The sad story is, I've gone to the retirement center and I wouldn't ask you to come and drive all the old folks beside themselves with your youngness."

"I'm sorry to hear that," Aunt Edna tells Marcella, touching her arm as briefly as a butterfly on a rosebush. "You must miss all the combustion of the grocery."

"Not a bit," Marcella answers. "I have my programs on TV, my card playing, and church on Sunday."

"How will the store ever get along without you?" My grandmother puts her palm over her heart as if stricken with worry.

"No store to get along," Marcella says. "Once

they put in that giant Kroger's supermarket, I lost most of my business—starting with the ones who owed me money." She seems at ease with this betrayal. I go back to her opening words: this woman *is* going to die, if not happy, at least at peace.

She digs into a large leather purse and comes up with a photograph, which she gives to me. "Your grandpa," she says, "around the time he met your grandma at that hospital she was resting at."

My grandmother doesn't like the detail about her once being sick, too, but she can't resist putting on her reading glasses, leaning over toward me, and admiring the picture.

"The handsomest man on two feet," she says, gazing at her husband who died long ago in the army. "Except for your daddy," she goes on, tapping my shoulder. "There was no one on earth to beat him in his younger days."

"That's a fact," agrees Marcella, and Mamaw nods in complete accord.

"Until now," Aunt Edna throws in.

They turn to her with confused expressions on their faces until she points to me.

I can't help it, I blush. I know compliments are like gusts of air in Kentucky—one waiting behind every tree—but I'm still not used to receiving them. When I look up, they're all smiling at me. My family: an old white lady, an old black lady, and a pair of middle-aged sisters.

I could stay in this moment forever. I could be whoever they want. I could fill in the hole in their lives that Dad made by leaving.

But, of course, I can't. Just like when he left Mom and me, the space is too large to ever plug.

chapter nine
chapter nine

DAD MUST HAVE FORGOTTEN ABOUT the three-hour time difference or simply not bothered to think about it, because when he calls to say Mom is getting out of treatment it's one o'clock in the morning and the ringing wakes up everybody in the house.

By the time Aunt Edna finally answers we are all clustered around her in the dining room. I'm treated to another one-sided conversation, except now it's Dad's voice I can't hear.

"Elgin!" Aunt Edna says. "Are you all right?"

We all lean forward in worry until she nods her head at us, listening hard.

"Ask him if he ever heard of sleep?" Mamaw commands, now that she knows it's not bad news.

But it turns out it is bad news—mixed, really. On the one hand, I get to go home to Seattle. On the other, I have to leave Louisville.

"I understand," Aunt Edna says, but her face looks like she doesn't understand a bit.

There's a long silence at our end.

"Don't be silly," she tells Dad. "It's out of the question."

"What is?" demands my grandmother.

"Sending our Rayona back on an airplane by herself," Aunt Edna answers without bothering to cover the mouthpiece.

"I *told* him that," my grandmother insists. "Distinctly."

"Well, if you can't find a way to come here and collect your own flesh and blood, then your mother and I will just have to gas up the car and bring her to you." She cocks an eyebrow in my direction as if to say, "That'll teach him."

"Of course we can," she continues after a break. "We used to take trips all the time. We'll alternate driving and Rayona can navigate."

Another pause while Aunt Edna studies the church calendar, framed by a blessed, braided palm, that hangs on the wall.

"Today's Saturday," she starts, then stops herself. "Excuse me, today our time is now Sunday. We can get a routing from the automobile club on Monday"—my grandmother nods—"and have her out there by this time next week if that will suit all concerned."

I wait, hoping for a clue about the condition of "all concerned," by which she means Mom.

"Then it will work out to a T," Aunt Edna says. "I have two weeks of vacation accumulated and Mama can certainly manage by herself for that long."

Without realizing I'm doing it, I move toward the phone. I need to hear Dad's voice to believe that Mom's well.

"There's a certain somebody standing right here in your pajamas who I *believe* would like to say hello," Aunt Edna says, and hands me the receiver.

"Dad?"

"Hey, babe. How you doing?"

"Is she okay? Really?"

"You won't recognize her. She's a new woman. AA, twelve steps, the whole works. She asks about you every time I talk to her but her doc says she shouldn't speak to you until you're here in person. He doesn't want a relapse."

Am I the one who made Mom sick?

"Ray?"

"Dad?"

"Love you," he says in that easy way of his. "Tell everyone I said 'Hi.'"

And then he's gone.

I replace the receiver on the phone. "He says 'Hi,'" I tell my grandmother and Mamaw, who are not pleased.

"I would have liked to hear my own child's voice." My grandmother's annoyance is directed to Aunt Edna, not me.

"Not even a 'How's Grandma'?" Mamaw wants to know.

"Oh yeah," I lie to her. "He did say that, too."

"A fib is still a venial sin," Mamaw advises me, but she's glad I at least tried to cheer her up.

We stand there, looking at each other, letting it sink in that I have to go. What's there to say?

"Let's raid the refrigerator," Aunt Edna proposes. "The way I see it, who's more entitled?"

On Monday, during her lunch hour from work, Aunt Edna, who is the official card-carrying member, goes in person to the automobile club and asks for a special favor. Since she's paid dues for twenty years and never requested such a thing before, she feels she's entitled to this as well, and when Aunt Edna believes she is owed something there is no denying her. She picks me up first and I go along for the experience.

"I need a routing to Seattle, Washington," she informs a young woman behind the counter. "Round-trip. Scenic route on the way out"—at this she nudges me with her elbow as if it's a private joke between us that I should understand— "and the fastest way home." She presents her membership card and the woman examines it.

"Summer is our busy season," the woman warns us. "It may take till Friday."

"The thing is," Aunt Edna says without changing her "entitled to" voice, "we're leaving at dawn tomorrow. I'm halfway through my lunch hour already. We'll wait."

The woman's eyes bug out. She's about to raise a million objections, then looks at the determined expression on Aunt Edna's face and surrenders before she starts.

"I guess you want the whole kit," she says in a kind of discouraged voice. "Triptik, tour books, marked maps."

Aunt Edna nods, says she's not about to set forth with her "precious cargo," as she calls me, without every scrap of paper her membership contract promises.

The woman sighs, is deflated, goes into a back room while we read posters about safe-driving tips and group vacations to Disneyland.

In less time than I imagine possible the woman is back with a fat bundle squeezed into a white plastic bag held together with a rubber band. "Have a safe trip," she says automatically, then adds, as an extra insider bonus, "beware of speed traps in Wisconsin."

On the way home we have one more stop to

make, a store that sells unusual used auto parts.

"We'd melt in the heat since your grandmother's car doesn't have air conditioning, just a vent," Aunt Edna tells me. "But there's this contraption I've read about—a cooler. You fill it with water, hook it to the roof of your car, hold it in place with a rolled-up window, and it blows a fresh breeze whenever you're in motion."

I don't question her. Aunt Edna knows what she knows.

The cooler turns out to cost thirty-two dollars and is shaped like a submarine. It's made of tan metal and comes with an instruction book.

"California, here we come," Aunt Edna sings as we drive home. "Right back where we started from." I don't point out that it's Washington where we're going. I don't want to spoil her good mood. I can tell she's excited at the idea of a long trip.

That night we study red line of the scenic route on the map—Indianapolis, dangerous Wisconsin, Minneapolis, a long stretch of the Dakotas and Montana. I have an awful moment of worry that they'll suggest we visit Aunt Ida on the reservation there, and some friend of hers named Dayton. He and my grandmother write letters sometimes—"To keep track of you since I never hear from your mother," she has informed me. I don't see how this is possible, since I haven't been back to the reservation since I was a baby, when Mom and I went to my uncle's funeral. I don't know this Dayton at all.

"There's no time for a family visit this trip," Aunt Edna decides.

This is fine by me.

"However," Aunt Edna says, "the house is not on fire. As a treat each of us can choose one place we're scheduled to pass near that she especially wants to see and we'll break the trip that way."

"I vote for Yellowstone National Park," my grandmother announces. "I've always wanted to see that geyser, Old Faithful."

"I put in for the Passion Play in the Black Hills of South Dakota." Mamaw, who is not actually going with us, does not concede her right to a choice. We will do this *for* her, for her sacrifice in allowing us to leave her alone, and then report back.

"What about you?" I ask Aunt Edna, who is staring at the map as if it is a candy display and she only has one quarter to spend.

"As long as we're in the neighborhood, I'll take Mount Rushmore. That mountain with the presidents' heads carved into it? It's right next to the Passion Play, so we can kill two birds with one stone."

Now they all look at me. What do I want to see between Louisville and Seattle? What's my heart's desire?

I realize it isn't a place at all.

"I've never been anywhere, so everywhere is fine," I say, but what I mean is I just want to be with you, wherever you go, and then find Mom at the end of the rainbow. Mom, well and herself, not too changed, is the sight I want to see, but I don't want to hurt my grandmother, great-grandmother, and great-aunt's feelings by admitting it.

"She just wants to go home to her mother," Mamaw says—once again performing her Vulcan mind-meld trick.

My job is to read the tour books, one for every two or three states, and suggest where we might stay each night, as well as to point out interesting facts along the way. I take my assignment seriously and scan the listings for motels that don't cost much but have swimming pools.

"Figure we make about four hundred miles a day," Aunt Edna suggests, and shows me how to read a mileage scale. Then she marks off likely towns: Madison, Wisconsin; Fargo, North Dakota; Rapid City, South Dakota; a long push to Yellowstone, where we'll take in the sights and spend the whole day; then Coeur d'Alene, Idaho, and . . . Seattle.

Luckily I find a cheap swimming pool in every one of these places.

"She's going to be a regular scientist when she grows up," my grandmother brags when I show her my list.

"An Olympic swimmer, more like it," Aunt Edna says. She herself is more interested in the words "coffee shop," and fortunately all of my places have those attached, too. That very night, because it's earlier in the west than it is in Louisville, Aunt Edna telephones all the places I've picked, plus the lodge at Yellowstone, and makes our reservations. No one has ever given me so much control, not just of my life, but of other people's. I feel like an equal partner, a member of the club.

Early next morning we load up the Mercury— suitcases in the trunk, filled-to-the-brim cooler attached firmly between the passenger-side window and the roof, picnic basket and thermos bottle in the backseat next to where I'll sit. When we're finished being busy, there's only one thing left to do, and nobody knows how to do it: say good-bye to Mamaw.

"Now that you know where we are," she says to me with a quiver in her voice. "Don't be a stranger."

"You take good care of yourself, Mama," my grandmother says, upset herself. "We'll call every night and report on our progress."

Aunt Edna doesn't say much but she looks as

though she's about to break apart with worry at leaving her mother alone. "You could come, too," she finally offers, but Mamaw shakes her head.

"I'm no traveler," she reminds them. "I get carsick."

We stand in a kind of box shape, the four of us, each at one corner.

Between themselves, I've noticed, they're no more easy with touching one another than Mom is with me—they've lived together too long for that, I think. So how do they manage a two-week parting?

"Come to your Mamaw," Mamaw calls me, and the square is broken, becomes a triangle. She smells of soap and powder and her cheek is as feathery as onionskin paper.

"Don't forget us," she whispers in my ear.

And then: problem solved. Aunt Edna is hugging *me,* who's going with her, from one side and my grandmother has wrapped her arms around me from the other. The square is now a big dot, a circle of arms and faces. With me in the middle, it's all right for my family to hold each other. I'm like the stem of a flower, one of Mamaw's prized peonies, and they're the pink and leafy petals.

"You could be a professional travel agent," my grandmother marvels after the second night. The motel in Fargo not only has a swimming pool and a coffee shop, but a special bed that pulls down from a wall so that we all get to sleep alone.

We don't talk a lot on the trip—the cooler is noisy, but if we open the window it will fall out so we make do without fresh air. With all the racket it makes, though, we quickly tire of saying, "I beg your pardon," when the thing one of us has mentioned isn't all that important. To fill the silence, we tune in local radio programs: farm reports, interviews with state-fair contestants, any kind of music except Protestant. Along with the clugging drone of the cooler we tap one another's shoulder and point to unusual things: a giant cow made out of hubcaps, a front yard filled with ceramic toadstools and dancing elves, a sunset with pink and purple clouds.

By the time we stop for the night my grandmother and aunt are worn out, ready to watch TV while I paddle around in the chlorine-filled pool. I never guessed, when Dad and I flew over all this in a matter of hours, what a long country it is.

The drive across South Dakota takes forever, without any change in scenery. It's as though we're going sixty miles an hour but standing still, or else, that same flat field, the same distant farmhouse, the same silo is matching our speed, going sixty miles an hour, too. When we finally get to the Badlands and ruts and crevices cut through the ground, Aunt

Edna is unimpressed.

"They don't look that 'bad' to me," she pronounces. "Naughty, maybe, but bad? I'll tell you about bad. Bad was the Ohio River flood in 1937."

"Ramona doesn't want to hear about that," my grandmother, who is behind the wheel and therefore, as she puts it, "the captain of the ship" declares, closing the subject.

I've gotten used to her screwing up my name and barely notice it anymore. It's like she has this mental block that keeps her tuned into familiar stations. Anything a little out of the ordinary irritates her. She rounds out odd things, like they teach you in school to do with fractions and decimal points. "Rayona" becomes "Ramona" because my grandmother once liked a movie with that title. Actually, my grandmother usually calls me Honey, Sweetheart, Dollbaby, or Sugarpie, which makes it easier for all of us.

But it's not just my name she rounds off. Dad becomes a "civil servant" instead of a temporary substitute mail carrier. Mom becomes "recuperating from a breakdown" instead of at a court-ordered detox. Aunt Edna is a "career gal" instead of a woman with a low-paying job who never married or had children.

"For heaven's sake, Marcella, I'm an old maid," Aunt Edna corrects my grandmother in mid–family story as we're driving below the speed limit some-where in Wisconsin. We are holding steady at fifty miles an hour. "It's not a sin."

"I'm an optimist," my grandmother replies in her own defense. "I've had to be." Somehow this explanation—which only puts more questions, like "Why?" in my mind, questions I know she doesn't want me to ask but to just imagine answers for that make her a heroine—has something to do with mix-ing up me and an old movie.

Finally we arrive at our first true "pleasure stop," as Aunt Edna has described the Black Hills. A whole twenty-four hours of rest, but of course we don't rest, we don't want to miss anything. We get into our motel in Deadwood at suppertime and hurry through the meal so that we won't let Mamaw down. Her trip wish was that we see and tell her about a reenactment of Jesus's betrayal, torture, and death, all performed each night by actors and actresses dressed up in Bible clothes. There's an out-door amphitheater with stone benches for the audi-ence to sit on.

I'm sleepy and would rather be swimming—I already know the plot—but I'm not allowed to doze off out of loyalty to Mamaw's one request. The guy who plays Jesus looks from the beginning as if he knows the plot, too—that no matter what he does or says, he's going to wind up crucified before he gets to rise from the dead.

Aunt Edna and my grandmother watch the play with the same expressions of attention on their faces that they wear at church. They hesitate before applauding the highlights, and it does strike me as strange: are we congratulating the actors for doing a good job, or are we clapping for God? It's almost midnight by the time it's all over.

"I found it moving," my grandmother says in the dark motel room before we go to sleep.

She gets no response.

"Edna?"

"Tourist trap." Aunt Edna's voice is as flat as the country we've been passing through.

"I'm an optimist," my grandmother insists, her usual comeback.

They're talking about more than the Passion Play, but I don't get exactly what it is.

"A person needs faith in this life," my grandmother continues.

"Real faith doesn't come cheap," Aunt Edna says to the night. "Real faith isn't something that charges money for admission. Real faith . . ." She pauses and I wait for her to go on, to tell me what real faith is, but she's finished talking.

"Every little bit helps," my grandmother says in order to have the last word and to let me know that we've had a good time and made Mamaw happy.

But as her words settle over the room, I can't stop wondering if she's right. Sometimes a "little bit" doesn't help at all. Sometimes it hurts. A "little bit" is what I was getting from Mom before she fell apart, and it turned out to be worse than nothing at all.

Aunt Edna is back to herself in the morning because today it's her turn to have a wish: Mount Rushmore, the faces of four presidents like a giant Jell-O mold on the side of a hill.

The road up to the Visitor's Center is steep, then we turn a corner and find ourselves staring straight into the face of Abraham Lincoln.

"It's a man-made wonder of the world," my grandmother approves.

We park the car and stand at the lookout. There's George Washington, Thomas Jefferson, Theodore Roosevelt. They remind me of those plaster of Paris casts Aunt Edna and I made on Sunday afternoons, except nobody's bothered to color them in.

"Well, say *something*," my grandmother demands. She has not forgiven her sister for criticizing the Passion Play in front of me, and wants an enthusiastic reaction.

"It just occurred to me." Aunt Edna is regarding the mountain with a sour gaze. "No women."

"Honestly!" My grandmother is losing patience.

"No a lot of things. There haven't been any women presidents."

"Exactly."

"Edna, you are going to drive me stark, raving mad," my grandmother says. "Nothing pleases you. And we both know why. You don't want to take Ramona back."

"Rayona," Aunt Edna automatically corrects, and I glance at her quickly, then look away. She thinks my name is important. What's more, I see my grandmother is right—Aunt Edna doesn't want me to go.

"Neither do I," my grandmother continues, and her voice is ragged, about to blow. "Into Lord knows what environment, our sweet darling."

Aunt Edna's face is not like one of the carved presidents: it softens, loses its set, responds to my grandmother's tone.

"Don't pay any attention to me, Marcella," she says. "I know it's just as hard for you. Harder."

My grandmother doesn't deny this but decides she needs to find the ladies' room. Aunt Edna says she wants to buy some postcards in the gift shop and asks if I want to tag along, but I shake my head, stay where I am. It's hard for me, too—that's what they're forgetting. A month ago I barely knew they existed and now it scares me to think of not having them handy. They make me feel safe.

I'm thinking this, looking out at the Black Hills, feeling sorry for myself, when a man says, "You're a breed, right? I can spot one a mile away."

I turn around and there's this middle-aged Indian guy in full costume—turkey feather headdress, buckskin suit, beadwork. I noticed him before—for a dollar he'll let people have their pictures taken with him with the Black Hills in the distance.

"My mom's an Indian," I say. I can't tell if he's being friendly or not.

"I knew it. I've been trying to figure you out, you and the two old white women."

I resent the way he says that.

"My grandmother and my great-aunt," I inform him.

"Right. Adopted?"

"No. They really are."

"And you believe them," he says. "They've got you fooled."

He doesn't know anything, this jerk, but he thinks he does.

"You know your language, your tribe even?" he asks to test me.

As it happens, I do know some Indian. Mom uses it to me around the house, especially when she's too impatient for English. Now I fire off one of her favorite expressions, one that she's made me promise never to say in public.

The man's face, surrounded by feathers, is surprised, amazed to hear words that aren't English come out of my mouth.

"What's that mean?" he wants to know. "All I speak is a little Crow, and that sounds more like, what? Arapaho? Gros Ventre?"

"It means you've got shit for brains," I translate for him. I'm breaking every rule in the book—saying those forbidden words, being disrespectful to an older person—but he has no right to put down my grandmother and Aunt Edna. No right to think he's figured us all out. Still, for Dad's sake, I add, "Sir."

An angry look clouds the man's eyes and I take a step back. I can see he's mad to have been wrong, embarrassed.

"Excuse me?" A woman with an I LUV GOLDEN RETRIEVERS T-shirt has come up to join us. "I was wondering if you're free for a photo?" she asks the man. She's holding out a dollar bill—the same George Washington face that is staring at us from Mount Rushmore.

The man sees me see, likes me even less, but this is work so he forces a smile, walks over, and puts his arm around the woman while her husband fiddles with the lens focus of his camera.

"Say cheese," the husband says.

* * *

92

The next morning we get up early for the long drive across Montana to Yellowstone and pass through the park entrance by four o'clock. The sound of the cooler must scare off the bears the travel guide claims are cruising around, but bears aren't why we're here anyway.

"I've always had an unnatural desire to see Old Faithful," my grandmother confesses. That's this geyser that blows hot water and steam straight up into the sky, regular as if it's attached to an alarm clock.

My grandmother, right after breakfast, can't get enough of it. "Imagine if everything was that predictable," she says to Aunt Edna. "Imagine if you could just live your life and be sure what was coming next, no surprises?"

"We've been doing exactly that for too long," Aunt Edna replies, but she too is fascinated by the burst of the hot-water jets. "We were in a rut, just like Old Faithful—until Ray came along."

They both look at me and smile, then turn back to the geyser.

"What are we going to do without her?" my grandmother wonders, as though I'm not standing there listening. "I feel ten years younger."

Aunt Edna fights her natural reluctance to keep her distance and briefly touches her sister's back. "It'll be all right," she says. "Now that we've made contact, we won't lose it."

"Yes we will." My grandmother will not be consoled. "That's what we always said about Elgin, and look at him. I'll bet we don't get a peek at her for another five or ten years."

Now they both stare at me, as if memorizing every detail. I don't know what will happen with Mom, don't know if I'll see much of Dad even though we live in the same city.

"I won't forget," I say, finally.

"Honey, it's okay if you do," my grandmother says. "Perfectly natural at your age."

"We'll remember you enough for all of us," Aunt Edna adds, and then, as if on cue, we turn our gazes forward, wait for Old Faithful to explode again. Standing between them, I slip one of my hands into one of each of theirs.

chapter ten

chapter ten

WE'RE ON THE NEXT-TO-last leg of our trip, driving on a deserted highway up into the panhandle of Idaho, and none of us is in a good mood.

Aunt Edna says something inaudible, and as usual my grandmother answers, "I beg your pardon," but Aunt Edna doesn't try again. A few miles later, from the backseat, I suggest we stop for a Coke.

"I beg your pardon," both Aunt Edna and my grandmother shout, and then, like Old Faithful, my grandmother blows her top.

"That's it! I can't take it another minute!" she yells, and with that she rolls down the window next to her. I watch, fascinated, as the cooler, released from its confinement, gives a little shudder, then lifts into the air and sails behind us, a Klingon ship on warp-five drive.

Aunt Edna brakes the car, stares in shock at her sister.

Out the rear window I can see the cooler skating down the empty road like a rock skipped on a pond. I turn back to stare at my grandmother, and it's as though everything about her, every color, has gotten deeper, brighter, as though she has been highlighted with a felt-tipped marker.

"There, I did it," she challenges Aunt Edna. "I opened the window. Sue me. I know, thirty-two dollars, hot weather to come." My grandmother has had an energy surge. She's Popeye after a can of spinach.

Aunt Edna hesitates for a moment before she speaks, then she says one of the best things I've ever heard anyone say.

"And high time, too."

My grandmother glances over to see if she means it, to see if Aunt Edna is actually furious under the surface. She isn't. Just the opposite.

"Everybody roll down the windows," Aunt Edna calls out, and steps on the gas. "All the way. California, here we come. Marcella, sing the song!"

Before, it seemed as though we'd been traveling in a sealed compartment but now everything—maps, Triptik, my loose long hair—is out and blowing, whipping around, moving in a stiff wind that enters the car from every direction. My grandmother's voice booms out at high volume. She hits every note, points at Aunt Edna, then at me, to join in, and we do, though none of us can carry a tune. We don't have to beg each other's pardon a single time more in the next two days. We don't care about the lost thirty-two-dollar investment, we don't care what we look like, we don't care if we're hot, we don't care if we're not even musical.

"Tell your mother you're descended from a pair of lunatics," my grandmother laughs, sounding like a girl.

"A pair?" Aunt Edna shouts back. "A whole long grizzly line."

Dad meets us at the LaQuinta Inn in Tacoma. He seems amazed to see us, surprised that we have actually done what we said we'd do and have arrived on time. He's dressed in his mail carrier's uniform and looks handsome like he always does.

"How'd it go?" he asks after kissing each of us on the cheek.

"We lost our marbles in Idaho," my grandmother says.

"She lost them," Aunt Edna corrects. "Your daughter and I just played along so we wouldn't be murdered in our sleep."

Dad wants to laugh at the joke but he's in the dark.

"It's okay, Honey," my grandmother tells him. "We're just teasing you."

"Mom?" I ask.

"She's all set up in a new apartment down in Parkland," Dad announces. "Close to her meetings, a new job at Denny's she can walk to. She looks good. She can hardly wait to see you. You get your own room."

"Are you there, too?" I ask, afraid to hear his answer.

"I'm in and out—you know," Dad says. "I go where the Post Office sends me."

"More in or more out?" Aunt Edna asks, but Dad just shakes his head.

"Do we get to say hello?" my grandmother asks. "After all these years?"

"Next time," Dad answers, embarrassed, and sneaks a look at me. "The doc says one adjustment at a time, and today I think Rayona is about as much as Christine can handle."

Nobody mentions we have just driven two thousand miles, and nobody challenges his decision. Nobody is surprised by it.

"Tell you what," Dad says to my grandmother and aunt. He sounds like a jolly weatherman on TV trying to cover up the silence that has dropped like an avalanche. "I'll just pop Ray over there and then come back here and have dinner with you all. Catch up. We'll call Grandma and have a nice long chat. How about that?"

I can tell that my grandmother and aunt don't expect a lot from Dad and so even this little visit is better than the nothing that might have been.

Aunt Edna turns to me. "I'm not going to give you anything to remember me by," she tells me, her voice guarded as if she has rehearsed this speech. "You'll have to do that on your own. You've got our phone number. Call collect. We never go anywhere, so we'll be there."

She steps back, giving my grandmother, in honor of our blood relationship, the last good-bye.

"I'll pray for you every night," my grandmother says, and slips a twenty-dollar bill into the pocket of my jeans. "You take your mama out to dinner on us and tell her someday we want to meet her in person." She pauses, swallows hard. "You tell her she's a lucky woman. You tell her she has a wonderful daughter, a prize."

Dad is looking away. This isn't easy for any of us.

Now it's my turn. They're all waiting, wondering what I'll say or do.

"I'll remember your grandmother's song," I whisper, trying not to cry because they haven't. "I'll remember Mamaw's recipes." I look straight at Aunt Edna. "Tell Cousin Marcella good-bye for me. I'll remember I have a brain in my head."

She doesn't drop her gaze, but it gets glassy.

I move to stand directly in front of my grandmother, who's holding Raggedy Ann for me to bring along. "I'll remember," I say, looking into her eyes that are Dad's eyes, wanting so badly to say something that will show her I really know who she is. "I'll remember you opened the window."

And then I run out the door, close my eyes, and promise myself that I'll never forget a thing, that I'll write to them. Send them school pictures and report cards and thank-you notes. But I know I probably won't and I know they'll understand.

"So, did you decide?" Dad asks, nervous, once we're in the car together.

"Decide what?" I string him along.

"You know, about the white thing. Telling your mom."

I don't know why it's so important to him for Mom not to know that he's part Irish. I don't know why that particular secret is his vitamin pill. All I know is that it's the one thing just between us, and that by itself makes it valuable.

"It's like the fish sandwich," I tell him.

"Come again?"

"You wouldn't understand," I answer him. "That's a secret between my grandmother and me."

He gives me a long look, thinks he gets what I'm saying, isn't sure, thinks again that he gets it, turns back to looking at the road. "You mean, you've got some secrets of your own now?" he asks.

I just raise my eyebrows and let him wonder.

"You didn't tell me all about your father, did you?" I ask. I'm guessing here, trying to fill in the blank space he left during our plane ride to Louisville.

Dad's eyes open wide, but he keeps staring straight ahead. "Did you bring up this subject with your grandmother?" His voice is level, like a fence around a house.

"I keep secrets real good," I reassure him. "Even ones I don't know yet."

His shoulders sag, relieved. A gate opens in the fence where there hadn't been one before. "You're something else, Rayona," he says. "One weird kid."

He makes this sound like I just got all A's on my report card, even in gym, but I wait him out.

"The thing is," he eventually goes on, "some facts don't need to come to light. They'd just complicate a person's grasp of . . ." He stops talking. He doesn't know how to avoid telling me.

"You don't have to." All I needed for now was for him to be willing to trust me all the way.

"Truly?" Dad brakes the car by the curb, puts his large, warm hand on my shoulder. "I'd rather let it keep, if that's all the same to you, till you're older. It's sort of a grown-up story."

That gets me even more curious than I already

was, but—and here's the strange thing—giving Dad the right to keep his own secrets is in an odd way better than hearing them. To know that I don't know something—as long as I get to know it someday—is like a promise between us. Respectful. Something nice people would do for each other, in a book, for instance, or on public television.

And as for the Irish stuff, it's not as though Mom's all that interested, since the idea has never occurred to her. If she asked me directly I'd tell her, I'm sure I would. But we've got so much else to talk about first.

As we turn the corner down the block I see that Mom is waiting by the front door of her building watching for us in the opposite direction, and she doesn't look a bit serene. I can tell she's nervous because she stubs out her cigarette on the sole of her shoe, then sticks the butt into a flowerpot so as not to litter. She's had her hair done in a different style that frames her round face in a space-suit cap of black curls. Her clothes are new, her makeup is fresh. She's gained weight. She looks a lot better than the last time I saw her—and for a second that gets to me because it doesn't seem fair. What right does she have to be so okay? Didn't she miss me, worry about me, lose sleep wondering how I was getting along? I've seen her sit by the telephone waiting for a date to call, and those times her face has been strained, tense, not sure of itself at all. Now, you'd think she'd been doing all that good-for-you stuff they preach about in health class—eating a balanced diet of the major food groups and getting enough sleep and following a regular exercise program. It's as though she has believed that I'd be fine during this past month, that perfect strangers would take care of me, that I'd be glad to see her when she was a new woman, and it really bothers me, watching her before she registers our arrival, that these beliefs have turned out to be— no thanks to her—one hundred percent right. When does somebody say, "Poor Ray"?

"Isn't she a sight," Dad says admiringly. "Prettiest damn woman I ever saw." He means it. He and Mom love each other in impossible but indestructible ways that have nothing to do with living together like normal people.

The feeling in his voice snaps at me like a rubber band, wakes me up to the fact that finally I'm back, that Mom is actually here, that I don't have to miss her anymore. I can breathe again, all the way down in my chest.

Dad stops the car, waits for me to get out, waves to Mom, and says to me, "You two have a good reunion. I'll head back to the hotel and make sure my mother and Aunt Edna are okay." He gives me one more hopeful look, waiting for me to promise, but I just smile. Then he drives off.

So there we are, Mom and me. Me frozen on the sidewalk, her on the front step.

"Oh, Ray," she says. "You poor little thing. I'm so damn sorry."

"It's okay." And it is. Mom's like one of those contestants on a quiz show who guesses the exact correct word to say and makes bells go off and all the lights in the studio blink. "Some of it was fun."

She isn't completely glad to hear this but can't say so.

"Can you forgive me?" she asks.

Neither of us have budged an inch.

"Sure."

"No, really."

I have the feeling Mom has gone over this moment with her counselor a lot of times, that she's sticking close to the advice she was given by some stranger who doesn't know anything about us.

"Really." I reach into my pants pocket, pull out the twenty-dollar bill. "Somebody gave me this for us to go out to dinner on her."

Mom looks at the money.

"Who?" she asks me automatically.

Here it is, the big moment, but it passes like a wave on the ocean.

"Oh, you know, one of the ladies I stayed with," I say.

"Was she terrible?" Mom wants to know.

"No," I answer. "She was nice to me. Just . . . normal."

"Normal" isn't something that grabs Mom's fascination, so she shifts her attention to what I'm holding. Her eyes light up for the first time. She has an idea.

"We'll have a feast," she decides. "I get an employee's discount at Denny's. We'll have dessert. The works." She's more at ease, stops twisting one of the rings she always wears, a silver turtle. "You hungry?"

"Starved," I say. "You?"

"I could eat a . . ." Mom searches her imagination for something big enough. "A banana split."

"Me, too."

"Ray," she says, then runs to where I stand, gives me one of her rare bear hugs. "I missed you so much."

"Me, too."

"It wasn't *all* fun?" Mom can't resist asking this question, can't help reassuring herself that nobody has come between us.

"No." I think of The Potters. "Some of it wasn't."

"I'm so sorry," Mom repeats, but she's mostly relieved. "I want you to tell me all the *good* parts." She means the bad.

"You know what?" she asks as she guides me into the building, presents me with my own key to the apartment for when she's at work, shows me my room, a mix of familiar objects and things that look as though they just came from K-Mart that morning.

"What?" I set Raggedy Ann square in the center of my bed, dig into my backpack, and plug Snoopy into a wall socket. Mom is tempted to say something but puts it on hold out of respect for our reunion.

Instead she taps out a cigarette from a pack of Marlboros, thinks better of smoking indoors, and carefully slips it back into the empty slot.

"I think," she says, her old self, her familiar happy voice, herself, herself, herself. Not "new" in any way that scares me. "I think we should declare today a national holiday."

"What'll we call it?" I let myself be caught up in her excitement.

"Rayona Day."

She smiles, waiting for me to smile back. I can't help myself. I do.

"Except this isn't just a once-a-year deal. This is from now on."

And I believe, as our dark brown eyes look into each other's, without any doubt, without any hesitation, without any holding back, that this time she really and truly means to try.